# The Whispering Window

## An Ethel Thomas Detective Story

# By Cortland FitzSimmons

Originally published in 1936

# The Whispering Window

© 2015 Resurrected Press
www.ResurrectedPress.com

## Published by Resurrected Press

This classic book was handcrafted by Resurrected Press. Resurrected Press is dedicated to bringing high quality classic books back to the readers who enjoy them. These are not scanned versions of the originals, but, rather, quality checked and edited books meant to be enjoyed!

Please visit ResurrectedPress.com to view our entire catalogue, and like us on Facebook at Facebook.com/ResurrectedPress to stay updated!

ISBN 13: 978-1-937022-98-3

Printed in the United States of America

# Resurrected Press Books in *The Ethel Thomas Detective Story* <u>Series</u>

*The Whispering Window*

*The Moving Finger*

*Mystery at Hidden Harbor*

*The Evil Men Do*

# Resurrected Press Books in *The Chief Inspector Pointer Mystery* Series

# RESURRECTED PRESS CLASSIC MYSTERY CATALOGUE

*The Uttermost Farthing: A Savant's Vendetta*

**Arthur Griffiths**
*The Passenger From Calais*
*The Rome Express*

**Fergus Hume**
*The Mystery of a Hansom Cab*
*The Green Mummy*
*The Silent House*
*The Secret Passage*

**Edgar Jepson**
*The Loudwater Mystery*

**A. E. W. Mason**
*At the Villa Rose*

**A. A. Milne**
*The Red House Mystery*

**Baroness Emma Orczy**
*The Old Man in the Corner*

**Edgar Allan Poe**
*The Detective Stories of Edgar Allan Poe*

**Arthur J. Rees**
*The Hampstead Mystery*
*The Shrieking Pit*
*The Hand In The Dark*
*The Moon Rock*
*The Mystery of the Downs*

**Mary Roberts Rinehart**
*Sight Unseen and The Confession*

**Dorothy L. Sayers**

*Anybody but Anne*
*The Bride of a Moment*
*Faulkner's Folly*
*The Diamond Pin*
*The Gold Bag*
*The Mystery of the Sycamore*
*The Come Back*

**Raoul Whitfield**
*Death in a Bowl*


*And much more!*
*Visit ResurrectedPress.com*
*for our complete catalogue*

*LIKE us on Facebook for upcoming release*
*announcements!*

*Facebook.com/ResurrectedPress*

# FOREWORD

From the beginning, Cortland Fitzsimmons proved adept at writing mysteries that tied into facets of the popular culture of the time. His novel *70,000 Witnesses: a Football Mystery* brought his talents to the attention of Hollywood when the novel was made into a film of the same name. This was followed by *Death on the Diamond: A Baseball Mystery*, *Crimson Ice: A Hockey Mystery* and *Sudden Silence: The Case of the Murdered Band Leader*. He also wrote mysteries involving the movie business and a professional magician. All of these novels involve a murder set against a background that was familiar yet exotic to his readers. That this was a successful strategy on Fitzsimmons part is evident in the fact that a number of these mysteries were made into movies and that he moved to Hollywood and became a screenwriter.

In *The Whispering Window*, he takes on another event that would have been familiar to most of his audience, a Sale Day at a major New York Department store. A fixture of the downtown of every major city in the country, the department store was an important feature of the urban landscape of the day, and major sales at such emporiums were well known to bring a crush of patrons looking for a bargain. What better scene for a murder, than the chaos surrounding such a sale where hundreds if not thousands of people were coursing through the store. Fitzsimmons takes full advantage of his setting, using not only the sales floor, but the vast support structure behind the scenes from the sub-basement to the top floor offices of the store management. And as familiar and commonplace as a store might be during the day, it becomes a much more forbidding environment after the customers have left and the lights have been turned off.

Into this landscape, Fitzsimmons introduces a most unlikely detective, the seventy-five year old spinster and part owner of the store, Miss Ethel Thomas. Thomas is no Jane Marple, tending to her knitting between solving crimes. She is a wealthy survivor of five decades of the New York social scene, a woman who was at her prime in the "Gay Nineties," but who adapted well to the "Roaring Twenties" and has managed to weather the "Great Depression" with a certain amount of style and elegance. But her age has brought her a certain amount of wisdom and experience with people as well as a sharpening of her sense of humor. She also has that indispensible skill for a detective, a keen observational sense. The fact that she has known the detective assigned to the case since he was directing traffic on the street corner outside her townhouse doesn't hurt.

The several mysteries in which Miss Thomas features are among Fitzsimmons best. While all of his books have a sense of pacing and snappy dialog that was tailor made for the movies, the Thomas stories have more depth and character development than some of his earlier works. This did not stop *The Whispering Window* from being adapted into the 1936 movie *The Longest Night*.

A note about the title of the book, which refers to a feature of the department store where a trick of acoustics allows conversations to be heard through a window in a balcony holding store offices. There is some evidence that Fitzsimmons had another title in mind. In one place in the novel he refers to the press calling it "The Bargain Day Murders," and in *The Moving Finger* there is mention of Thomas having written a book about the events called *The Department Store Murders*. And of course, as mentioned above, the movie was entitled *The Longest Night* referring to the period after the store closes where the puzzle is solved. It is not clear, then, whether the title was Fitzsimmons choice, or something suggested by his publisher, not that such things ever happen.

Though during the span of his career, Cortland Fitzsimmons was both a successful author and screenwriter with nearly twenty novels and nearly as many screen plays to his credit, including at least four adaptations of his own work. Yet today, he is relatively unknown. It is therefore with great pleasure that Resurrected Press presents this new edition of *The Whispering Window*.

**About the Cover**
The cover of this edition incorporates re-worked elements of the original dust jacket used on the first edition of this book, published in 1936.

**About the Author**
Cortland Fitzsimmons was born in Brooklyn, New York (possibly Queens) on June 19, 1893 and died July 25, 1949 in Los Angeles, California. After attending New York University and The City College of New York, he worked for some time as a salesman for several book distributors and publishers before turning to writing full time in 1934. Most of his works as a writer were mysteries, a number of which were based on sports themes such as *70,000 Witnesses: A Football Mystery*, *Crimson Ice: A Hockey Mystery*, and *Death on a Diamond: A Baseball Mystery*. A number of his novels were made into films and he moved to Los Angeles to work as a screenwriter. His last book was a cookbook that he co-wrote with his wife Muriel Simpson *You Can Cook If You Can Read*.

Greg Fowlkes
Editor-In-Chief
Resurrected Press
www.ResurrectedPress.com
Facebook.com/ResurrectedPress

# CHAPTER ONE

If young Charlie Doane hadn't called on me that Thursday night I'd have missed one of the most exciting experiences of my rather checkered and eventful life. I've had adventures, all sorts, but Charlie's visit was to be my introduction to murder, though neither one of us knew it at the time.

It was the next morning that my lust for crime detection was born. I've read about murders in the press and books, but to see a victim right before your eyes is an entirely different matter. My house was robbed once and I can still remember my burning rage as I went over my things to see what had been left to me. I had that same hot uncontrollable rage as I looked at poor Mrs. Briggs. I wanted to get the person who had done that monstrous thing and throttle him with my own two hands. I was a one-woman lynch riot all by myself.

At seventy-five, and more or less in my right mind, my interest in young men is put down as a maiden lady's whim. At thirty-five I was called a rather reckless old maid, and when I was forty they didn't have a name for me. The common use of the term "Bachelor Girl" hadn't been invented then. I've always liked men with a preference for the younger ones. My reasons for never marrying are my own business, but now as I look back on my life, I do feel that I would like to have had a husband—but that, as a young man once said to me, was a pluperfect wish and no man is that good. Perhaps the young lad was right. I haven't missed the man at all, but there is something about being called Mrs. Something or other which sounds infinitely more satisfying and fulfilled than being plain Miss Ethel Thomas. As you probably have guessed, I'm known as a character. Heaven knows what they would have called me if I hadn't been born to wealth and a social position in New York.

I had always liked young Doane. Even as a blond, long-legged, rather skinny boy I had found his down-right straightforwardness interesting. I admired him for that quality. I have it myself, but it took years of training people and family before I could safely ignore all the social dictates that keep most people hidebound, particularly women. Being born to a position in society with your name in the Social Register is a responsibility if you're not society-minded. But what I think or what I'm like has nothing to do with the story except as it may explain my part in the unraveling of the strange and horrible murders which the press so delighted in calling "The Bargain Day Murders."

As I said, my part in the weird business (weird and horrible it was, but I enjoyed every minute of it) came about because Charlie Doane called on me that night before the yearly Doane Sale. If you know anything about New York at all you know that the Doane Sale is one of the biggest bargain merchandise events in the entire country.

If you were born to wealth as I was and were fortunate enough to have your health and live as long as I have, you just can't help having more money than you know what to do with. There I've ended a sentence with a preposition, but I can't help it. If I'm going to tell this story, it'll have to be in my way and prepositions, split infinitives and the like can go hang. Perhaps I'll get away with it just as Will Rogers did, bless him! I wonder if they'll call me quaint.

To get back to my money. It is important to the story. Uncles and aunts and cousins kept dying, possessed of that strange idea that money must be kept in a family. Their kindness kept adding a bit here and there to my already substantial fortune, making it necessary for me to find new and better investments each time I received another legacy. Money is a responsibility. If you want to keep it, you have to work for it. I realized that when I was reasonably young. Among other things, I have been called a smart business woman. I was always on the lookout for a good investment (I have to be) and when Charlie Doane came to me five years ago and made me a proposition, I accepted it.

Charlie hated the store and all the details of its management, although he did stay in it until his father died. At Robert Doane's death we, who were in the know, could see no reason why Herbert Hastings, who owned twenty-five per cent of the stock and had been acting president and general manager, shouldn't go on in that capacity. I certainly knew that Charlie didn't want to be tied down with the responsibility of the position. Herbert went into the store after he married Charlie's sister Gladys, a prissy, empty-headed woman if ever I saw one. Herbert had some money and bought into the store, which pleased everybody at the time. It was 1921 and in the light of what has happened since, no one remembers that period as a depression, but I do because I can remember how skittish money was at the time.

Robert Doane's will divided his fortune more or less equally between his two children. I suppose it was a matter of pride, family name and all that sort of thing which prompted him to leave the store stock as he did. Herbert already owned twenty-five per cent of the stock. In the will Robert left Gladys enough shares to make the Hastings family forty-eight per cent owners. To Charlie went the remaining fifty-two per cent, so that store control would still belong to the Doanes. Men have queer ideas about their names, wanting them to live and be known; but, then, that was Robert's business and he was so like the run of the mill as far as business men are concerned that I needn't single him out for my criticism.

Soon after the estate was settled, Charlie came to me and offered me twenty-five per cent of his holdings in the store. He didn't say so, but I knew he felt he could trust me. I liked his genuflection to his father's wishes because between us we would still control the store policy; and the name of Doane, for better or worse, would go down in department store history. Charlie's reason for turning over his stock to me was a personal one. He wanted to go cavorting around the world; and I didn't blame him. When a man has as much money as he wants I don't see why he doesn't have a good time instead of trying to make more.

Charlie was known as a most eligible bachelor. I often wondered why he didn't marry. I asked him once and he said he'd fallen in love with me and all other women suffered by comparison. A man who can make speeches like that shouldn't be allowed to run around loose. If I had been younger or if I had known a man like Charlie when I was a girl—

I will ramble, but when your head is full of so many things I suppose it's natural. To get back to my deal with Charlie. It was a silent one. Charlie wanted my cash and I took his stock. We didn't make any legal transfer. He took my money, I took a part of his stock and put it in my safe deposit box, where it was, if and when it was needed. Dividends were paid to Charlie, who transferred my share to me. It was a nice arrangement which suited us both. At the time the store was making money. It was a good investment.

Dividends began to fall off after the depression finally convinced some of the men, who should have known it at the beginning, that it was here to stay, but I didn't worry about that. I live simply—or at least I think I do for a woman of my income. I like my house and I like well-trained servants. I entertain a great deal. I'm too old to spend money in any other way, and so a partial depletion of my too large income didn't worry me at all. When you own a proper home and take care of it, you don't have a great deal to worry about. I have enough silver, linens, crystal and that sort of thing to carry me through a number of years before I could be called frayed gentility even if things get worse than they are. That time won't come, however, because I have bought annuities enough to keep me going even though the bottom falls out of everything. I'm not worried about the annuities, because if the insurance companies fail, we'll all be in the same boat and I guess I'll be able to take care of myself. I wasn't even worried that night when Charlie came, his face as dark and glum as ever I had seen it. The darkness came, I realized later, from his long sojourn in the South Seas, but the glumness was because of the store. He was worried more for me than for himself—though goodness knows it was enough to worry him. He fancied himself as one of those bad men who cheat helpless women and children out of their money. I have been called 'most everything during the course of my life, but Charlie was the first one to even intimate that I was defenseless, I who have always enjoyed a good fight no matter what the provocation!

Charlie, like so many other men, was on the verge of ruin. Being down there in the South Seas for so long, he had no idea of the frightful things happening to our finances. It was a letter from me which brought him home. I didn't bother to write him for nearly a year, but when two dividend periods passed with no word from him I wanted to know why. I thought he had forgotten to transfer the first dividend, but I knew he wouldn't let two go by without letting me know why. If he needed the money for himself, all he had to do was say so. When he received my letter he became worried and started for home. He found himself practically wiped out and the store stock worth next to nothing.

"Isn't there any business at all?" I asked.

"Yes," he answered thoughtfully, "there seems to be a fair amount of business." He answered my question and then went wool-gathering. Charlie's thoughts were off somewhere and I didn't propose to sit there wanting information while he did a bad imitation of Rodin's "Thinker." He was sitting on a stool in front of me, his elbow on his knee, his good firm square chin cupped in the palm of his hand.

"Come, come, Charlie!" I scolded. "Don't sit there mooning like a young calf. It doesn't become you. Collect what thoughts you have and bring them out into the open. I take it you came here for help or advice or both."

"I did." He shifted his position and looked up at me. I'd do a great deal to save him from a hurt of any kind. I rather think what little maternal instinct I have has centered itself in Charlie. When you can't have a man for a husband, you'd like to think of him as a son. I feel that way about Charlie.

"Well, are you going to tell me or will I have to drag it out of you? If the store is doing business, why are you on the verge of ruin?" I demanded.

"That's what puzzles me," he said seriously. "I haven't been back long enough to get the proper picture. The store is teetering on the edge of collapse. Business has been fairly good for depression years, but there have been no profits for some time and it is beginning to go into the red. When a business starts downhill, it slides rapidly unless something is done quickly," he ended hopelessly.

"Where are your losses?" I demanded.

"Generally, all over the store," he replied.

"Haven't they tried to reduce overhead?" I asked impatiently, feeling certain I knew how to remedy the situation.

"Salaries have been cut. We're operating with a minimum staff. All that sort of thing has been done," he explained.

"Doesn't your accounting system show the vulnerable spots?" Not being in business, I sometimes think business management is very stupid.

"The books seem all right. I've been going over them. That's one of the things which bother me. I think we ought to get in an outside accountant for a complete check-over."

"Why don't you?" I asked. "I've always believed a good diagnosis is more than half the cure."

"Herbert doesn't think we should spend the money,"

he replied.

"Herbert, indeed!" I snorted. "He's always been penny wise and pound foolish."

"He's been running the business while I shirked my responsibility," Charlie reminded me.

"What are you going to do about it? Just sit there and let the whole thing go to pot?"

"I guess we'll have to borrow money." He said it dolefully. "That is, if I can hypnotize some bank president."

"Which means you will have to give up the store control. It will be a Doane store in name only, is that what's worrying you?" Before he answered, I went on, "You don't want outside interests in there, do you?"

"No, I don't. I've always hated the store. You know that. At the same time I've been proud of it, and, by God, I'm not going to let it get out of my hands! I'm not going to sell out and I'm not going to lose control. It was my job and I ran away from it. Now I've got to go back into harness and patch up, if I can, the mess my neglect has caused."

"Now you're talking like Charlie Doane. Go to it!" I was proud of him then. For a moment I had thought the straightforward go-getting young man I had liked had been jellied by his stay in the South Seas. I'll admit I was thinking of the South Sea sirens down there as contributing to the softening influence.

It was at my suggestion that we decided to have a meeting the next morning with Herbert and tell him of my interest in the store's finances. I could have offered Charlie money enough that night to carry him and the store over a bad spot, but I didn't want to do it, because I think it's a mistake to relieve a man of a sense of responsibility if he has one. There are plenty of them these days without it, goodness knows. I suppose women must be to blame for the crop of men I see running about; they usually get blamed for everything anyhow, but this time I think justly so.

"I can't redeem the stock I sold you," Charlie said sadly. "I've spent all my money, investments have gone to pot and my interest in the store isn't worth a cent at this moment."

"Who said anything about your redeeming my stock?" I snapped. "I'll lend you more if you need it. For yourself," I added.

"But I can't have you losing money because of me!" he protested.

"I bought the stock from you, didn't I?" I asked a bit more savagely than I had intended.

"Yes."

"I bought it because I thought it was a good investment. You're not man enough to put a fast one over on me. I knew what it was worth at the time. You didn't make this depression. As a matter of fact, if more of our leaders had done what you did or jumped off a cliff, the depression wouldn't be half as bad as it is now. I can take a licking if I have to. I'm in on this Doane deal with you and I'm going to see it through to the end. You don't want outside interests in the store. You have considered me as being one of you. We'll see what is to be done to-morrow after we have a talk with Herbert. The first thing to do is to put our finger on the sore spot. When we've located the ailment we can worry about the cure."

"If you mean you may be willing to dump more money into the store," he said, "the answer is No." His dander was rising.

"I'll protect my investment in any way I think fit. Think that over." I hurled that at him, filled with determination. The young scamp telling me what to do! I liked it, but I wouldn't let him know it. Even a bossy woman likes to have some one with grit enough to tell her what to do.

Charlie had been thinking over my suggestions and finally said, "To-morrow is a bad day. You know what a Doane Sale is like. Every man, woman and child in the store will be doing the work of two people."

I didn't know anything about a Doane Sale. I knew they had them—you couldn't help it if you read the papers—but what it might mean to the store I had no idea. "Sale, fiddlesticks!" I said. No, I didn't say that at all; I swore. "Hell and damnation," were my actual words. I put the fiddlesticks in because I think that this might one day be published. I suppose every one thinks he can write a book. I've heard people talk about it, and while I know my friends think my occasional cussing is cute, quaint and a lot of other descriptive adjectives instead of a form of expression, I did feel that an editor, something gray and drooling perhaps, might think it wasn't just nice. I've only met one editor and he was a dreamy, impractical, head-in-the-clouds young man who, if he wasn't, shall I say odd, certainly suggested lavender. If I was a nice old lady I don't suppose I'd know anything about pale young men, but then I do read a great deal and I can't help seeing what I see.

I assured Charlie that, sale or no sale, our business was important and in the words of our President the time for action was at hand. I fancied that our troubles were over, at least the discussion of them, and settled back for a friendly chat. I was wrong. Charlie's mind wasn't free for a chat. There was something else bothering him. He had something he wanted to say and he didn't know how to go about saying it.

You've seen children, servants and men fumbling about, doing a mental teetering on the brink of a disclosure of some sort. That was Charlie. I've little patience with the attitude of mind which engenders such an uncertainty. When I want a thing I ask for it. When I have something to say, I say it and devil take the consequences.

He was vague, answering my attempts at conversation with monosyllables. I wanted to hear something about the South Seas, but I could get nothing out of him. I gave him chance enough to speak and when he still evaded the issue I pounced on him.

"What have you done?" I snapped. "Robbed a bank, raped a virgin, or murdered an old lady for her false teeth?"

He smiled a sickish sort of a grin and came out with it. "It's happened," he said.

"What?" I asked, knowing full well what he meant.

"I've fallen in love at last."

I gave the news time to sink in. I knew he'd like me to be impressed. Why are people so shyly ashamed of being in love? I've been in and out of it a hundred times and have always felt a divine exultation over the experience. It's just like playing solitaire—you always hope the next time will work out without your stacking the cards.

"Who is she?" I asked after a proper interval.

"No one you know." He still evaded a direct answer. I knew I'd have to drag it out of him, so I went to work. "Did you meet her traveling?"

"No."

"Then, where did you meet her—pick her up on the street?"

"It's a girl at the store," he said, a trifle nettled.

I was surprised at that. It seemed just a little cheap to me, but for once I didn't say anything.

"You'll like her," he assured me. He had probably read my thoughts.

"I hope so." I couldn't keep the emptiness and hurt out of my voice. I was losing something and I couldn't do so without regret.

"It's not what you think," he said defensively.

"I'm not thinking," I retorted.

He swung round on the stool and put his chin on my knee and looked into my eyes. "She's a grand girl, Ethel. I think she's beautiful and good. She has everything." His face glowed. When a man talks like that the case is hopeless. He went on. "I've haunted the jewelry department. I've been nice. I've invented excuses just to talk to her. I've done all the things a man can do to make a woman aware of him."

"How long have you known her?" I asked.

"I don't know her at all. She won't let me. She has a 'Hands off' sign in evidence all the time."

"She would if she were a nice girl," I defended. "She probably doesn't trust you."

"But I—"

"She doesn't know your intentions are honorable," I teased.

"I neither look nor act like a roue, do I?" he demanded.

"Love at first sight, eh?"

"I guess so. She's the only girl in the world for me."

"And she's giving you no encouragement?" I asked without any effort to conceal my skepticism.

"She doesn't give me anything. She doesn't even know who I am."

"If you think any employee in the store doesn't know you, you're crazy," I retorted.

"There's no reason why she should," he protested.

Bats may be blind. I don't know about that, but they certainly have nothing on a man in love.

"Except that you own the store," I reminded him caustically.

He paid no attention to that, but went on with his mooning. "Why didn't I meet her before?" He certainly wasn't asking me that question. "Why does it have to happen now when I'm as good as broke?"

"She'll probably be satisfied with you as you are," I suggested.

"I'd like to give her everything."

"Do you want a wife," I asked tartly, "or something to dress up and show to your friends?"

"A wife, of course."

"If she's the right girl, what you have will make no difference."

"I'm sure of that, only I'd like to be able to do things for her."

"Why don't you wait until you learn something about the girl?" I suggested.

"I know I want her. What more is there?"

Of course I had no answer. We let it go at that. I gave him several drinks of my very best brandy, but that only increased his glumness. He was worried about business and he wasn't at all sure that he'd be able to get the girl. He was considerably mellowed as he said goodnight and told me he was determined to put the store on its feet and get the girl at the same time.

"To do or die for them both," I teased, having no idea how close to death he would be.

# CHAPTER TWO

I was supposed to be at the store shortly after nine the next morning. Punctuality has always been one of my virtues, I think, but a vice and a terror to my friends. I can see no excuse for wasting another person's time and I have no patience with people who are habitually late and take pride in what, to me, is a most inconsiderate shortcoming. I've never waited more than fifteen minutes for any one and I doubt that I ever will. When I say shortly after nine, I mean not more than ten minutes past the hour. I manage my time; I suppose that's why I'm not late for appointments. Malcolm, my chauffeur, had his order for the car and called for me at eight forty-five. We were singularly lucky with the traffic lights and pulled into the side drive of the Doane store several minutes before nine.

For the first time in my life I really saw what a store sale meant. Malcolm had difficulty getting the car into the old carriage drive at all. I never saw so many nondescript women herded in one spot. They were jammed about the entrance, milling and chattering, crowding and shoving, fighting for position. Malcolm turned his head with that look which always asks a silent question. His expression was contemptuous. He's really an awful snob.

"I'll sit here until they get inside," I said, knowing he would feel relieved. He does like to take care of me.

I was fascinated by what I saw. There were hundreds of women of all sizes and shapes. I've seen pictures in the so-called humorous magazines of the crowds at a sale, but this was my first at-hand experience. My Lincoln is an old model and therefore rather high from the ground. Long ago I discouraged smart young salesmen with the new-car-a-year-and-save-money idea. A car is good as long as it runs, and I have no desire to be zoomed over the country in one of those new doodle-bug models which are cluttering the streets at the moment and are advertised as being smart. Jules Verne and H. G. Wells should have thought of them years ago along with their other weird notions.

From my lofty seat I could see the crowd. Pressed close to the door was a round, red-faced, rather jovial-looking Irish woman. That is, she was jovial until a portly, black-wigged Jewish woman by skilful maneuvers almost succeeded in obtaining Ireland's position. It was a battle of races and I didn't want the doors to open until I had seen the show finished. Several tired females had squatted on the running-board of the car and one of their children with sticky fingers was climbing on the rear fender to get a peek inside. Malcolm was annoyed and gave me that look of his, but I shook my head to quiet him.

The little bout being enacted in front of me made me think of "Abie's Irish Rose" and the Cohens and the Kellys.

This particular Mrs. Cohen had edged herself into a position beside my Irish friend. I'll admit I was prejudiced in favor of the Irish woman. I don't know why, but I liked this Mrs. Kelly and was placing my bets on her. She looked a person who did things openly and with determination. A quality I've always admired.

With a wiggling of hips and shoulders (I've seen it in the subways) Mrs. Cohen forced Ireland a bit to one side. Just as I was wondering what Redface would do, out went the Kelly elbow in a vicious poke and although I couldn't hear it, I'm sure Mrs. Cohen grunted. Ireland had regained her position directly in front of the door, where an attendant stood ready to open up. I sat back. I was sure of Ireland's supremacy in anything resembling a fight; but I think we were both lulled into a sense of

security by her momentary victory. I sank back against
the cushions. We had both underestimated the enemy, for
just as the door was about to swing open I saw Mrs. Kelly
wince and jerk to one side. From her actions I am sure
that the Cohen foot must have planted itself on an aching
Kelly corn or bunion. At any rate, Mrs. Cohen was swept
into the store first and victorious, while poor Mrs. Kelly,
fighting for her position, milled about in the crowd. Like a
wave of water spreading itself over a flat plain, the eager
women vanished in the aisles of the store. Malcolm
opened the door for me and as he did so I caught him
scowling at the child's fingerprints all over the rear of the
car.

"What on earth!" I exclaimed as the blaring strains of
a band smote my ears. I looked into the street, thinking
to see one of the pre-war German bands. They played
horrible music, but they were picturesque and a part of
the life that once was New York. "Is there a parade
somewhere?" I asked as Malcolm took my arm. He always
handled me as if I were something brittle which he
expected to break apart at any moment.

"No, madam. It's music in the store. Customary, I
believe, on Sales Days." His disgust for the rabble which
had just left us was obvious in the pained tones of his
voice.

"Don't wait," I said, and then unable to resist teasing
him a little I added, "unless you want to do some
shopping."

"I patronize the small shops," he informed me
prudishly.

"I'll telephone or take a cab." I turned from him.
Malcolm has a way of running me, and every once in a
while I have to assert my independence. He hates to have
me ride in cabs, keeps insisting that they are not safe,
while I find the drives interesting and many times
exciting, particularly Sixth Avenue on a wet afternoon.

As I stepped into the store Peterson, the doorman,
smiled and greeted me cheerfully. The band was on a

platform in the center of the main floor and was making a terrific din. A few feet ahead of me Mrs. Kelly was standing, a bewildered expression on her florid face. I had somehow not thought of her as ever being bewildered. I don't know what prompted me, unless it was a feeling for a kindred soul, for I guessed what her trouble was by the way she clutched at her skirt on one side. I stopped and asked,

"Is there something I can do for you?"

"I can't hear a word you're saying, for that damned band!" she shouted.

I had to shrill at her over the trumpeting of the band. "Is there something I can do for you?" I repeated.

"There is not," she replied with a rich brogue, "unless you're after having a safety-pin and an extra garter hidden about you somewhere. I've broke the both of them trying to get in here."

She was clutching her side, and having been in a like position I wondered why she did not do what I'd have done in a similar predicament. It's simple enough to let your petticoat fall to the ground, step out of it and roll it into a small wad. But, then, I've never been called modest in that false use of the word. I was chuckling as I said I was sorry, and for the poor woman's benefit I pointed to a door a few feet from us. She waddled toward the sanctuary, still gripping at her undergarment. I could see no trace of a falling stocking. At the door she turned and winked at me, an inclusive friendly gesture, opened the door and vanished from my sight.

I have always been the first to laugh at people who resort to bromides and trite phrases as a means of expression, but, darn it all, they do have their place. Trite as it may sound, it is the little things which are important. There, I wanted to say exactly that. If I hadn't arrived early and witnessed the bout between my Mrs. Kelly and Mrs. Cohen the store murders may have gone down in history as unsolved crimes. As unimportant as it may seem, the mere fact that I stopped and spoke to that poor woman, distressed as only an inherently modest soul can be embarrassed, was to be very important later on. Not because I knew the Doane family but because it was in itself a very satisfactory store, I had always liked to shop there. Then, too, the fact that the clerks, the older ones, knew me helped, I suppose, to flatter me. My Christmas list for the Doane employees had always been a large one. From the moment I passed the ever-vigilant Peterson at the door until I reached the particular department I was bent on at the moment, I was always greeted with glad smiles, and I don't believe it was just because at Christmas I was something of a Lady Bountiful. I have always tried to remember that in the scheme of things we are all human beings, some of us more fortunate than others due to the possession of worldly goods. I don't hold with the near-sighted philosophers who say that money isn't everything. It isn't, I'm willing to admit, but the mere fact of having money, enough of it, does give you a sense of security and the courage to do things which otherwise you might not dare venture. Money, of course, can't make a person happy. No one thing can. Happiness, like the measles, must get its start from within. I've lived a full and, to me, happy life, and my money helped, there can be no question of that.

After leaving Mrs. Kelly going through that door, I continued along the aisle. I had to cross the main floor to the elevators in the corner, which were the ones I always used when I went as high as the executive offices.

I'll take a minute here to describe as much of the main floor as we need know about. As you enter the store from the side entrance, which I always used, on your right you pass several feet of paneled wall. I never thought about it or knew what was behind that wall until I was so precipitately thrown into the excitement of that day. The door toward which I had directed Mrs. Kelly was in this walled area. On the left, opposite the walled space, and beyond the balcony stairs, was the hand-bag section. Next to it was the jewelry department; and on the other side of the jewelry there was a counter of women's handkerchiefs. The buyer of that department knew my weakness and kept an eye out for me. Whenever she had a bit of Honiton or Carrickmacross lace she knew I would like she usually sent it home on approval.

I stopped for a moment at a table in the book-shop, which is just across from the jewelry department. There is always something in a book department to catch your eye, and Mrs. Curtis at Doane's certainly knew how to catch my eye—also my purse. Right smack on the aisle in front of me was the most intriguing display of cook books and kitchen gadgets I've ever seen. I don't profess to be a cook, but I do like food and am continually buying cook books and kitchen gadgets for my cook, who accepts them placidly, and rarely, if ever, uses either the new-fangled contrivances or the books. She doesn't need them, really. I suppose it is the woman in me coming out, after all.

I was intrigued by a new type of food-grater which guaranteed no bruised knuckles—when the scream came, cutting across the general hubbub of the store. It was so unexpected and so agonized that for a moment chills ran down my spine. For a fraction of a second the noise in that great store died away while ears were cocked to locate the direction of the sound. I never realized before that you can't tell the direction from which sound comes. I had no idea and, like the hundreds of other women on the floor, I looked about to see a crowd gathering at some one spot. There was no commotion anywhere in the body of the store. Clerks queried one another with their tired eyes. The momentary hush was engulfed in the resumption of routine noises. I saw a clerk from the book section go through a door which was a right-angle continuation of the paneled section flanking the lobby. The band began to play. The store resumed its busy tempo.

It was ten minutes past nine. I looked up at the clock. I should have been in Charlie's office, but I didn't go toward the elevators, for at that moment the man who had slipped through the partition from the book department reappeared in the door and beckoned. His face was white and he looked so helpless, as only a man can, standing there, that I felt his call for help was directed toward me. It wasn't, of course, but nothing could have held me back.

I reached the door directly behind Mrs. Curtis, who was too intent on what she was doing to notice me.

"What happened, Clayton?" Mrs. Curtis asked crisply. I have the greatest admiration for that woman. She was always busy and I don't believe she had time to read much of anything, but she knew about books and, most important of all, she knew the books I liked to read. Furthermore she never, if she felt it, showed any intolerance for my rather catholic taste. She sold me love stories, mysteries, biographies and anything else that I happened to want and did it as if each one was the most important book in her stock. I can't abide opinionated book clerks who have such superior taste that they make you and your preferences seem less than the dust.

Clayton—I have never learned whether that was his first or last name—was at the gulping stage and said, "It's Mrs. Briggs and Miss Oliver."

"Both of them?" Mrs. Curtis expressed the surprise which I myself was feeling.

"Yes, ma'am. Miss Oliver is on the floor and Mrs. Briggs is hunched over her desk paying no attention to Miss Oliver."

"Did you call the infirmary?" Mrs. Curtis asked. He showed clearly that he had not. "Do it," she ordered and went through the door. I followed.

Behind the partition there was a narrow corridor which ran the length of the paneling. I noticed three doors opening from the side of the narrow passage and one at the extreme end which I thought must have been the door through which Mrs. Kelly had vanished for major repairs. As I followed Mrs. Curtis to the center door of the series I could hear the store signals bonging out their calls for executives. Perhaps you have noticed the sound. Suddenly you hear bong, bong, then a pause and then two or three more bongs. That is a system used by the telephone operators when they want to locate an important person in the store. Each executive has a different signal.

I suppose you are thinking, "Why doesn't she get on with the story?" I merely mentioned the call signals because had I gone to the executive offices I would have missed both Charlie and Herbert, for they were at the moment being summoned to the main floor.

Mrs. Curtis stepped into a small office. I was directly behind her. Clayton's description had been brief and adequate. Mrs. Briggs was most certainly hunched over her desk in a strange posture and Miss Oliver was still prone on the floor. Never in my life have I seen a woman equal in size to Mrs. Briggs; that is, outside of a circus, where one expects to see freaks.

Mrs. Curtis knelt beside the girl and put a be ringed hand on her brow.

"Just a faint," I said. "She's coming out of it now. I saw her eyelids flicker." If Mrs. Curtis was surprised to see me, she didn't show it.

She stood up and said, "I never faint myself. What does one do?"

"Pat their wrists, dash cold water on their faces, lift their legs up to get the blood back to the head, or just leave them alone," I replied. I was more interested in the Briggs woman. I didn't know what her trouble was, but I felt certain that whatever it was, she was the reason for the Oliver girl's scream and subsequent fainting.

Mrs. Briggs' body was against the desk. Her head seemed to squat on the mound of flesh which was her body. Undressed she must have looked like a series of inflated inner tubes. One fat, ham-like arm was on the top of the desk. It was her hand I noticed—although fat and chubby, it was smallish and cute. I always notice nice hands. Her nails were well-manicured, and in noticing them I spied the small bottle which lay on its side with the poison label turned up.

"Look!" I cried, and pointed at the bottle.

Mrs. Curtis gasped and the next moment was making the sign of the cross; an automatic gesture, I'm sure, but one which impressed me at the moment. I saw several other things in those few seconds while the commotion in the corridor warned us that others were approaching. In front of Mrs. Briggs there was a golden chalice and trailing from her hand I saw a broken string of golden rosary beads.

They all seemed to come at once. A uniformed nurse who knelt beside Miss Oliver; Herbert Hastings looking very much the stolid, getting-heavy-around-the -jowls business man; John Grover, his second in command, bustling, loudish in dress, red of face and full of action; Charlie, with that steadiness about him which was a relief to me; young Sandy McLeod, red-headed, blue-eyed, freckled and as Scotch as good oat-cakes.

"What happened, Mrs. Curtis?" Herbert asked, taking no notice of me, surprised or otherwise.

"I don't know. There was a scream. Clayton came in here and then called me. Miss Thomas came with me. I think Mrs. Briggs"

While she was talking, Charlie came and stood beside me, his hand reassuringly on my arm. Not that I needed help or protection, but there are some things a man does that endear him to the hearts of women. Charlie was like that—thoughtful, protective and considerate of all women.

The nurse was between Miss Oliver and us. Herbert and John Grover were at the desk, stepping over the body of Miss Oliver to get there. Sandy McLeod walked around her and I liked him for it.

It was Herbert who finished Mrs. Curtis' speech. "She's committed suicide," he stated, and in his voice I read resentment, criticism and annoyance. He might just as well have said, "How dare she do it here on a Sales

Day!"

The nurse shifted her position. We had a full view of Miss Oliver. I felt Charlie's hand tighten on my arm for the fraction of a second. There was a tense worried look in his eyes as he left me and knelt beside the girl, who was regaining consciousness.

I knew then. He didn't have to say a thing. There was a possessive tenderness in his every muscle as he bent over her.

# CHAPTER THREE

You can't live as long as I have and be unfamiliar with death. One of the greatest penalties exacted from those of us who live to an old age is the losing of friends and intimates by the natural processes of elimination. The older you get, the greater the price. Death has always awed me. It is so devastatingly final, such an end to everything. I love life. Perhaps that's why I have always felt sorry for people who found life so unattractive or so difficult that they thought they must end it. I was made reverent for a moment by the most unexplainable of mysteries—suicide.

Herbert's speech annoyed me. Suppose the poor soul had ended her life in his store on one of his Sales Days? What of it? She had spent most of her life in the store; it was probably more a part of her than anything else she had ever done. If she was tired of living, I think she picked the proper spot, sale or no sale. I felt like telling him so, too, and probably would have done so (another of my weaknesses which people have grown to condone; they say I have a sharp tongue) had not John Grover spoken at that moment.

He turned to Sandy and said, "Get a stretcher and keep the crowd away. They're beginning to herd in the book department and we can't have that."

The store, nothing but the store. There was no real thought for that poor woman except perhaps by Mrs. Curtis, who seemed genuinely moved, Charlie, who had sympathy for everybody, and myself.

"We'll have to take her out the back way," Sandy said suggestively as he viewed the bulk of her body.

"Get the stretcher! We'll take care of that," Herbert said impatiently.

Sandy was off to a telephone in the next office. Mrs.

Curtis, with a glance at Miss Oliver, who was being reassuringly held in the nurse's arms, followed him.

"What happened to her?" Miss Oliver asked.

It was the first good glimpse I had had of the girl. She was lovely to look at. A creature of breeding and culture, you could see that, and in any position except flat on her back I'm sure she'd have had poise and dignity. No woman can look her best just coming out of a faint, flat on her back in a cramped office. I knew what Charlie meant. I knew why he felt about her as he did. For a moment I was intensely jealous. I suppose a mother feels that way about her sons. I liked the look of the girl and resigned myself to the idea of Charlie loving her. Charlie was bound to love and marry some day. He was far too normal to die a bachelor.

"There now, dear," the nurse soothed with that assuring tenderness which only a good nurse or a mother lulling a fractious child to sleep can manage.

"Is she dead?" Miss Oliver asked insistently.

At the nurse's nod of affirmation, Miss Oliver sighed deeply.

"Come up to the hospital and rest for a while," the nurse suggested.

Miss Oliver sat up. "I can't." She tried to stand. "I'll have to keep my eye on the department. The clerks will be upset. There's so much to be done."

What gets into store people? There she was, just after a terrific shock, probably a mass of quiver inside, thinking not about herself, but the store, as soon as she gained full possession of her faculties. For a moment I suspected her of making what the boys call a grandstand play; but what followed made me a little ashamed of myself.

I could tell by the look in his eye that Herbert approved of the young lady's attitude. He was mentally licking his chops. It was Charlie who stepped into the gap—-

"The department can take care of itself for a half-

hour. I want you to go with the nurse. That's an order."
He was short about it and bossy, but kind with it all.

I fancied I saw a smirk steal across the faces of both
Grover and Herbert, but I'm not sure.

Miss Oliver seemed doubtful about Charlie's authority
and looked questioningly at first Herbert and then John
Grover for confirmation.

Herbert grudgingly said, "Mr. Doane is right, Miss
Oliver." Then he spoiled it by saying, "You'll need all of
your energies later, so it's best you take a brief rest now."

The girl was assisted to her feet by Charlie and stood
for a moment while the nurse smoothed out her clothes.
I've had nieces and young cousins galore in the course of
my life, but I've never seen any person, even a Thomas,
who suggested the perfect thoroughbred so well as Miss
Oliver did standing there. I couldn't take my eyes away
from her. I didn't blame Charlie one bit for falling in love.
She wasn't just pretty or beautiful; it was something fine,
a sense of quality that glowed about her. If she had an
aura, I saw it as she stood there. For a moment I envied
her her fine smooth skin and soft golden hair. I was
momentarily ashamed of my own blonde wig, one of my
so-called idiosyncrasies. I made up my mind to see more
of that girl—provided, of course, she would permit it. It
wasn't just because of Charlie. I wanted her to like me for
myself. I'd have made the effort for any woman Charlie
wanted to marry and I wouldn't have cared much one way
or the other, but this girl was different.

I racked my memory for Olivers I might have known
in the dim past. Stephen Oliver was the only one I could
recall. He was an idle man-about-town, of good family,
who never did anything remarkable except to marry some
chorus girl and retire to Italy, I think it was, and live as a
remittance man for the rest of his life. His family had
been shocked and ashamed, but Stephen wouldn't give up
the girl. I admired him for his courage at the time, but
that must have been fifty years ago.

Charlie and I watched her as she started to go. His

eyes were expressing openly the admiration he was feeling. She had just reached the door, still under the protecting care of the nurse, when John Grover stopped her.

"Miss Oliver," he called, "just a moment. You knew her quite well. Is there some one we could notify?"

Miss Oliver stopped. "She has a son, Carl Briggs," she replied.

"And where can I find him?" Grover asked.

The girl started to speak. She made a sound which would have been a spontaneous reply to the question had she finished it. You've heard people start a word and cut it off. It was an R sound and I had the feeling that she was going to say Regent and give a telephone number. Her eyes flickered for a moment before she went on with a statement which was good enough but was not what she started to say the first time. It all happened very quickly and perhaps if I had not been so interested in her looks, I'd not have noticed it.

She said, "Right beside the telephone, there is an address book."

I like people who can think quickly. I've known a few rascals in my time who did it very well, both male and female. I'm not accusing Miss Oliver of being a rascal. Her reply was an evasion of some sort and the reason for it intrigued me. My positiveness may have been an old woman's fancy or it may have been intuition, for I've told many a lie to evade an issue.

The nurse urged her out of the room. As they left I turned to Charlie and said, "Fine-looking girl, don't you think?"

I've had lots of experiences, but when it comes to love at first sight I must admit I'm a bit skeptical, because it doesn't take into account such things as table manners, speech and disposition. But of course I wasn't surprised when Charlie said, "She's the only woman I've ever seen who is capable of being your rival." He squeezed my arm affectionately. Perhaps now you understand why I like

Charlie Doane. A dozen Irishmen who had kissed the Blarney Stone as many times could not have said anything more charming. Few men have the wit or the ability to pay a compliment to one woman when they are enthralled by another. Imagine at seventy-five being compared to something young and lovely! I was thinking beyond the compliment when Herbert exploded impatiently,

"Why don't they come with the stretcher?"

"How about the police?" Charlie asked. "We'll have to notify them, won't we?"

"Later," John Grover muttered. He was preoccupied, pushing a blotter back and forth along the edge of the desk. He made me think of a small boy playing with a train.

Outside, that confounded band went on playing. I suppose it did lend a tone of gaiety to the sale and probably helped to keep people quiet after the scream. Music does calm people, I suppose, but there is music and music and a department store is no place for a concert.

There were only four of us there then—Herbert, Charlie, John Grover and myself, and of course the dead woman. It suddenly occurred to Herbert that I didn't know John Grover. He acknowledged the introduction with some asinine remark about being sorry to meet me on such a sad occasion. He had about as much compassion as a blood-thirsty fan at a prize-fight.

Herbert added to my annoyance by saying, "I didn't expect our conference to be like this."

Grover was peering about at the top of the desk. I suppose he wanted to see if the woman had left any important work undone.

"Don't be an ass all your life, Herbert," I snapped, completely out of patience with both of them.

John Grover guffawed, Herbert blushed and Charlie's eyes seemed to say " 'Atta girl." People do egg me on, you know. I didn't know then that the three of them had raked me over the coals a few minutes before. Charlie told me about it later. It seems that John Grover and Herbert didn't want me in on any store conference. Charlie insisted—I had to drag that out of him—that since I held twenty-five percent of his stock I could not and would not be ignored. It was Grover who said that since the stock had not been transferred I could be counted out. Charlie explained that he had said some terrible things about me to the effect that even if he was willing to do anything as shabby as that, they were reckoning without a full knowledge of me, my temper and love of a good battle. I don't know, Charlie didn't say, but from looking at John Grover, I'm sure he called me "the old dame."

Sandy and two pasty-faced, thin-shouldered young men came in with the stretcher at that moment and I found myself wondering how those men were going to be able to carry away that mountain of flesh. No one had tried to find an address book, because the woman occupied the entire front of the desk and I'm sure that none of us were interested in even attempting to move her.

Fred Banter, who was head of the personnel department, came in all out of breath, his face beaded with perspiration, to see what had happened. He was accompanied by a man they called Kramer who was head of the store detectives. He was my idea of a detective, heavy and dull, with shifty eyes and an expression about the mouth which resembled an incipient snarl. He spoke in short gruff sentences which I imagine was his idea of being efficient and businesslike. They stepped to one side while a short explanation was given.

"Now you won't have to discharge her, Mr. Doane," Banter said.

Charlie flushed at the remark and said, "Providence has a way of taking care of things."

The young men went to work and handled her very well, I thought, only they didn't get her properly on the stretcher and when they tried to lift her, her head lolled back with sickening looseness.

"Wait a minute!" It was Sandy who spoke and in his excitement I detected a slight burr.

"Get her head on the stretcher!" Grover commanded.

"It's not that." Sandy was on his knees on the floor beside the woman, who had been lowered back.

"You're only delaying things!" Grover snapped. "Let the men get on with their job!"

It seemed unduly heartless to me, that speech, but then nothing is important in a store but the store. I was glad Sandy stuck to his guns.

"It may be important," he insisted. The two men couldn't move the body until Sandy was out of the way and he didn't budge.

We were all interested in what he was doing. I know I was. With his fingers he was smoothing out the flesh of her neck, which was nothing more or less than several rolls of fat.

"What are you doing?" Kramer asked impatiently.

"Look!"

Sandy directed attention to her neck.

There was a dark bruised ring about the woman's throat. Sandy's quick eye had discovered something which we all had missed. The implication was obvious, but Charlie surprised me by asking,

"What of it?"

"I think, sir—" Sandy's words just wouldn't seem to come.

"What the boy means," I said for him, "is that the woman has been murdered, choked to death with—" my eyes went to the broken string of rosary beads on the desk, "that golden chain."

Naturally they didn't want to believe me.

"It doesn't seem possible," Charlie said doubtfully.

"It can't be," John Grover denied.

"Come now, ma'am," Kramer said, and for less than two cents I could have slapped his heavy face.

"But the poison," Herbert said, for all the world like a

small boy who hates to give up an established idea.

"That's ridiculous!" Banter objected. "Who would want to kill old Briggs?"

"We'll have to call the police now," Sandy said.

"Keep out of this, McLeod," Kramer barked. "Get back out there on the floor where you belong."

Sandy did as he was told. He was a nice lad, but no match for his gruff superior, though I'll bet Sandy had ten times as much brains.

The matter-of-factness of the others annoyed me. Why on earth didn't they do something?

The two young men with the stretcher were, I thought, singularly unmoved by the bomb-shell which had been exploded in our midst. If one of them had nonchalantly lighted a Murad I'd not have been surprised.

Herbert, who was beside the desk, peered into the chalice. What he expected to find I've no idea, but he was very satisfied with himself as he turned to the rest of us and said,

"There's poison in there. She must have taken it. The mark on her neck is probably from a string of beads or a necklace."

"Then where is the necklace?" I demanded. "And look at her lips." I pointed down at the flaccid mouth. "Wouldn't they be burned if she had taken poison? Furthermore, is there a mark of her lips on the cup?"

Up to that time Herbert had not touched the chalice. Prompted by my words he reached for it and was halted by Charlie's serious voice saying, "I wouldn't do that if I were you. Fingerprints are important."

Herbert's hand went back to his side as if he had been stung.

"This is a fine mess!" Grover muttered.

"On Sale Day, too," Banter said. "It'll be a bother with the police interrupting our work. I don't suppose we can—"

"Why didn't you post a sign in the store this morning,"

I snapped, "warning murderers to wait until the sale was over?" They made me sick with their old store and sale.

"Better call the police," Charlie instructed Kramer, . who hesitated a moment, looking from Grover to Herbert.

It was Grover who nodded.

Kramer went into the next office. We could hear his harsh voice coming over the top of the partition. The band was quiet at the moment. I'm sure we all had the same idea as Kramer's voice came to us distinct above the rumble of the store itself. Why hadn't some one heard the murderer?

# CHAPTER FOUR

Charlie has always said that he'd rather have my luck than a license to steal. Being born rich rather than poor is luck and something over which we can have no control. I've been lucky, I'm willing to admit, and it was a piece of luck that I should happen to know the detective who was put in charge of the case. On the other hand, my knowing him was not luck at all. Peter Conklin, the detective, had once directed traffic at the corner of my street. As I told you, I've always been interested in men. Peter was a young man when I first saw him shivering on the corner in the cold January wind. I found him pleasant and agreeable always. Being a person who doesn't mind her own business exclusively, I stopped one day to speak to him. He had a shock of curly black hair (I saw that when he removed his hat, contrary, I believe, to regulations), dark laughing eyes and a slightly snubbed nose. At various times I bought and gave him such things as ear-muffs and gloves, to say nothing of the coffee and, perhaps I shouldn't mention it here, good liquor which I instructed my cook to give him whenever he appeared at the service door. Peter and I were the best of friends while he was on the beat. He was promoted about three years ago and I had lost track of him until I saw him taking charge in Mrs. Briggs' office. When you have lived as long as I have, done and known the things and people I have, then perhaps you will have the same kind of luck. I certainly wouldn't have known as much about the case if it hadn't been for Peter and I'm quite sure no other man would have allowed me to interfere as much as he did. Call it casting bread on the waters if you like.

While the others were waiting for the police to arrive, which took about fifteen minutes, I walked through the store, thinking about the murdered woman. I have a friend who calls all mystery stories Who-done-its. I was asking myself who and why as I roamed up one aisle and down the other. The store's bustle of business went on without interruption. The band played intermittently. Except for the clerks in the book, stationery and jewelry departments no one in the store seemed to know that there had been a tragedy. One death couldn't interrupt the routine of a great store. Business had to go on. Tragedy and heartache could be played against its rumble, but couldn't stop its voice. The show had to go on.

As I passed the religious counter at the end of the book department, where all sorts of things of interest to Roman Catholics were on display, I saw my Mrs. Kelly involved in the purchase of a plaster Madonna and a thirty-nine-cent rosary.

"Do you wish them sent?" the clerk was asking as I drew near.

"Of course. Do you think I can be lugging that statue around without breaking it?" Mrs. Kelly retorted.

I moved up beside her. She gave her name and address before she saw me. "Mrs. Patrick Doyle, 47 Petticote Road, the Bronx," she said and then asked, "Will I get them to-morrow?"

"I think so," the girl replied.

"Don't you know? Macy's do it," Mrs. Kelly offered scathingly.

She didn't know that mentioning Macy's in any other New York store was like waving a red flag at a bull. I knew it because I'd heard old Robert rave and rant so much.

"I'll mark it Special," the girl promised.

"You'd better." It was then that Mrs. Doyle turned and saw me. "It's you," she said. "You saved me life."

"Not that bad, surely," I returned with a smile.

"Well, when you're all coming apart as I was and not knowing what's going to go next, it's pretty bad," she said.

I'll admit I was at a loss for conversation.

"Have you been looking around?" she asked. "It isn't

much of a sale. I came down for the house dresses they advertised, and I wouldn't be seen dead in one of them." She took her change which the girl handed to her and said, "The rosaries are a bargain if you're needin' one," and left.

My mind went back to that little office. What was Mrs. Briggs doing with the chalice and rosary and why the poison? Had she intended to commit suicide, after all? It didn't make sense. If there were some one I wanted dead and I found him in the act of taking his own life I'm sure I wouldn't hasten matters and complicate things for myself by killing him. Such questions were milling about in my mind as Mrs. Doyle trundled away from the counter.

I was loitering over the biography table in the book department when Sandy came to tell me that the police had arrived. Herbert and Grover both had felt certain the police would want to question me, as I was one of the first at the scene of the crime. The police were at work in the little office, scads of them intent on their jobs. There was a doctor examining the body of the poor woman, photographers were setting up their cameras, fingerprint men were already at work at the desk and a young man with his back to me was examining everything in that room. Charlie and the others were huddled in a group near the door, watching. I peered over their shoulders to see what was going on. I've read about such things in books, but this was the first time I had ever seen the police in operation. The young man in charge turned round.

"Peter Conklin!" I exclaimed.

"Hello, Miss Thomas!" he said, grinning at me with that bond of fellowship which had always existed between us. He took off his hat, which up to that time had been cocked on the back of his head. "What are you doing here?" he asked. "I've always thought it would be fun to pinch you."

"Try it," I challenged, very glad to see him again.

At that moment the doctor, who was very intent on his work and I'm sure had no sense of humor, spoke to Peter. "I can see no trace of poison on her lips or in her throat," he said. After that had sunk in, he went on, "The condition of her eyes and tongue doesn't indicate death by strangulation."

"Then what did kill her?" Peter demanded.

"I can't tell, but from this brief examination I believe the pressure on her throat frightened her to death. I'm sure her heart stopped. I can tell more later. As soon as the photographers have finished I'll take her away and give you a full report."

"How do you think she was strangled?" Peter asked.

"Cord or wire," the doctor replied matter-of-factly, "probably applied by some one she knew very well."

"Wasn't it the chain?" I raised my voice to ask.

The doctor gave me a contemptuous look.

"Would that be possible?" Peter asked.

"Too frail," the doctor replied. "She undoubtedly had the rosary in her hands when the strangulation started. I believe she broke the beads herself. I found a small piece of the chain in her left hand."

There was the first of my theories gone to pot, but I had to admit, as I thought about it, that the doctor was probably right. Poor soul. Had she tried to pray even as she was being murdered? She was evidently a righteous woman.

Peter looked at the small bit of chain and grunted. Then he went back to his inspection. He was here, there and everywhere in that small office and I marveled at his movements. He never once got in the way of the others who were doing their work. Peter stopped behind the chair in which Mrs. Briggs had been sitting and thoughtfully rubbed his chin. He turned, faced us and looked at the long narrow table strewn with odds and ends, which was directly behind the chair. Some of the things, I suppose, were samples. There were boxes, some correspondence, a stack of bills and another pile of papers which I took to be orders waiting to be sent out.

I heard the fingerprint man grumble about the lack of prints on the desk. "The desk's a blank," he said to the man working with him; "been rubbed."

Peter was down on his hands and knees inspecting the floor near the wall at the end of the desk. He looked like a diligent hen scratching in the dirt. When he stood up he had some small ends of wire, a piece of black tape and some frayed cotton, all of which he deposited on the narrow table.

"How often are these offices cleaned?" he asked.

It was Grover who replied, "Every night after hours."

"Then this mess," Peter pointed to the litter of his findings on the table, "was made this morning?"

"Probably," Grover replied. I'll find out." He instructed Sandy to call the repair department.

"All ready," one of the photographers announced.

Peter asked us to go into the next office and wait. The next room belonged to Mrs. Curtis and I found it a fascinating place. I follow the *Times* "Book Review" and "Books" of the *Herald Tribune* carefully and knew that most of the books in that office were not yet published. There were a few galleys, some paper-bound advance copies and other books not yet on the market. I'd like to have taken a half-dozen of them away with me.

An officer stuck his head into the door and said, "I can't locate the girl who fainted."

"She's in the infirmary," I said, wondering why some of the men didn't speak up.

"That's where she isn't," the officer replied.

"Find her!" Peter snapped. The man withdrew.

Sandy returned, accompanied by a man in blue overalls which were full of interesting pockets and loops from which suspended a hammer, a screw-driver, a pair of pliers and other things I couldn't identify. He looked like a gadget tree.

"Were you in Mrs. Briggs' office this morning?" Peter asked.

"I fixed a call-button for her," the man replied.

"At what time?"

"About ten minutes after eight."

"Any one else in there?"

"Miss Oliver was in and out of the office for a few minutes," the man answered.

"What's the button for?" Peter asked.

"It connects her office with the wrapping desk in the jewelry department and was put in to save the old lady steps. She had trouble getting around. I did most of the work last night and finished up this morning," the man explained.

"Did you leave any wire behind?" Peter asked.

"I don't remember," the man replied. "There may have been some small bits. I don't know."

I imagine electricians are something like plumbers and leave their tools here, there and everywhere, though how he could with that fascinating suit of his with a place for everything on it, I don't know.

"Outside of Miss Oliver, was there any one else in here while you were working?"

"A mail girl came in, and then just as I was finishing, her son came."

That was a surprise to me. Was that why Miss Oliver had hesitated when asked about the son?

"You know him?" Peter asked.

"Naw," the man replied. "He said, 'Hello, Mom,' when he came in. I was finished then and left."

As the electrician was leaving, an officer came in with Beth Oliver, who was dressed for the street in a neat fall coat and a most becoming hat.

"She was just coming in," the officer announced with the satisfaction of a captor in his voice.

Just a short time before I had heard her say that she had to take care of the department. Why had she suddenly decided to let the store take care of itself? As she faced Peter there was something lurking in the depths of her eyes that I could not fathom. She was calm and poised as she waited for Peter to begin. Where had she gone and why?

"Why were you out of the store, Miss Oliver?" he asked.

"I wanted a breath of fresh air," she answered.

"How long were you gone?" he went on.

"Just a few minutes," she answered.

"She got out of a cab," the officer cut in.

"Fresh air in a cab, Miss Oliver?" Peter had a cute way of making a question-mark by arching his eyebrows.

"Yes; I had the windows open."

"The driver said he picked her up on Fifty-first Street," the policeman offered.

I wondered how he had learned so much in such a short time and decided that Peterson had probably identified the girl. I discovered later that my guess was correct.

"You walked up and rode back?" Peter suggested.

"Yes, I did," she agreed, somewhat relieved.

"You worked for Mrs. Briggs?" Peter went on.

"I was her assistant."

"You were the one who found the body and screamed?"

"Yes."

"It must have been a shock." She didn't make any answer to that. He went on. "We expected to find you in the hospital."

"I didn't go there," she answered. From what I saw of it later, I didn't blame her.

"You rested in one of these offices, I believe?"

"In this one," she answered.

"How long did you stay here?"

"Just a few minutes. I couldn't sit still, I couldn't rest. I had to move about. The store seemed stifling; I decided to walk."

"Do you know of any reason why Mrs. Briggs would want to commit suicide?" he asked.

"No."

"Can you think of any one who would want to murder

her?" was the next question.

"No." Her voice was so low I could hardly hear the answer.

"Tell us what you did from the time you entered the store until you found the body," Peter suggested.

Peter's stenographer's pencil flew over the paper as Beth talked.

She began with directness and told her story calmly.

She arrived at the store at five minutes past eight. That statement surprised me. I had no idea that people in department stores had to do an hour's work before the store opened. No wonder they are so tired and listless in the late afternoon. The hours seem much too long.

Mrs. Briggs had been cross with her for being late, she said. There was no resentment in the girl's voice as she said it. From what followed I gathered that the Briggs woman was something of a martinet. Beth Oliver—I always think of her as Beth now—said they had worked until nine the night before getting ready for the sale. Another fact which surprised me. Certainly one half of the world doesn't know how much the other half works. Laugh at that if you will; I know it's bromidic, but it's true. I glanced accusingly at Herbert, but of course my censoriousness made no impression on him.

On her arrival that morning Beth did a few odd jobs in the office, called the repair department to see why the call-button had not been installed and then went to the stockroom to see that everything was in readiness there for the day's sale.

"Didn't you come back here at all?" Peter asked her then.

"Once," she replied.

"Why?" he asked.

"I found a small bag of rhinestone jewelry tucked away behind some boxes," she answered.

"Was that so important?" he asked.

"It seemed so to me."

"Explain, please." He sat back waiting.

"For some time," Beth continued, "we have been having shortages in inventory."

"Just what does that mean?"

Herbert broke in to explain, though I'm sure Beth could have done it. The gist of what he had to say was this: Their sales didn't cover the stock which they had bought. In other words, when they bought a hundred dollars' worth of merchandise and sold half of it they should have fifty dollars in cash and fifty dollars in stock. They didn't. They had the fifty dollars in cash but not more than thirty dollars of stock. He said they had checked and rechecked their inventory, but were unable to locate the shortages.

"I understand," Peter said to stop Herbert's continuance with a list of store figures. He turned back to Beth. "This bag of jewelry. Why did you bring it down?"

"I have believed that our shortages were due to theft. The jewelry I found had been taken from the department, as it was already marked for sale. It was the first tangible evidence we had had that things were being taken out of the store by employees."

"Did you suspect any one person?"

She hesitated, reluctant, I imagine, to accuse any one.

"What did Mrs. Briggs say about it?" Peter didn't make an issue of It.

"She was talking to her son and didn't say anything. I put the bag on the table, explaining where I had found it, and went back to the stockroom and stayed there until I heard the opening bell."

"Didn't Mrs. Briggs make any comment?"

"She just nodded," Beth answered.

"Then you and she had talked about shortages before?"

"Yes."

"And you did suspect some one?" I wondered when he would come back to that question.

"We suspected every one," she answered.

"You sound like a policeman," Peter grinned at her.

"Didn't you have anything tangible?"

"We talked about it last night," Beth answered. "For some time I have been watching the department and one girl in particular. I suggested last night that Mrs. Briggs let the girl go."

"Why?"

"I have found her trays badly arranged, her stock scattered in different places and once or twice I discovered little piles of easily concealed items. I believed they were segregated on purpose."

"You reported those things to the store detectives?" Peter asked.

"I told Mr. Kramer. He watched the girl, but we could never catch her stealing."

"That's right," Kramer confirmed Beth's statement.

"And the girl?" Peter ignored Kramer.

"Mrs. Briggs was going to dismiss her this morning."

"Did she do it?"

"I don't know."

"She didn't." Banter stepped forward. "She'd have to do it through me. There were no complaints to-day. Probably due to the sale." He smirked.

"Mrs. Briggs was murdered," Peter said brutally. "Do you think this girl—" He didn't finish the question, because Beth interrupted.

"But I thought—" Beth hesitated. I was sure she was acting.

Peter repeated his question. "Do you think the bag of jewels you found may be connected with her murder?"

"I shouldn't think they were valuable enough for murder," she answered.

Peter turned to Herbert then and asked, "Do you know offhand the shortage figures in the jewelry department?"

"In the past year," Herbert replied, "it has run into several thousands of dollars. A really terrific loss, enough to keep the department from making money."

"Then the amount was large enough to warrant

murder; that is, if Mrs. Briggs knew the thief."

"Exposure would mean jail," Herbert pronounced.

Peter digested that for a moment and turned back to Beth.

"Who is the girl?"

"Must I?" She asked the question of all of us.

"Speak up, Miss Oliver," Grover urged.

"Eva Sutton," Beth said.

"And now," Peter went on. "What were you doing on Fifty-first Street?"

"Walking," she answered quickly.

"Are you sure you didn't go up there to see, say, Carl Briggs?"

"Quite sure," she replied. I saw the color drain out of her face, if Peter didn't.

# CHAPTER FIVE

I was wondering why Peter had asked that question about Carl Briggs. He evidently knew something which had escaped me. I'm sure I'd have been as uncomfortable as the girl was had that calculating stare of his been turned on me.

"Tell me about the finding of the body," he suggested with a smoothness I didn't exactly trust.

"When I first entered the office," Beth began, "I thought she was sleeping."

"Sleeping?" Peter asked quizzically.

"Cat-naps," Beth explained. "She was very touchy about them, too," she went on. "I bustled about the desk doing a few odd jobs trying my best to make enough noise to waken her."

"You didn't see the bottle of poison?" Peter's question contained more than a modicum of doubt.

"When I entered the door I thought she was sleeping, as I told you," Beth continued her explanation. "She didn't like to come out of a doze with any one watching her. I didn't look at her again for several minutes. I was expecting her to say something to me. It was a game which we have been playing lately. When I finally looked, wondering why she had not spoken, I saw the bottle. I must have screamed then. I don't remember anything else until the others were all in here."

"You believed it suicide?" he asked.

"Yes."

Peter sat back, digesting what she had said.

Her story sounded true enough and Peter seemed satisfied. I wasn't. That girl was holding something back. If she sat in one of the offices next to the death room she probably heard everything that was said by us when we made our startling discovery of the murder. Another thing. I was sure when she left the office to rest that she had no intention of leaving the store.

Why, then, had she left the store? Was it because sitting in the room next to us she had heard our talk and exclamations when Sandy uncovered the murder? She must have heard us, because when Kramer left us to telephone the police we could hear his sharp voice so clearly. Beth, if she hadn't been caught just as she was returning, intended to keep her little walk a secret. I was certain of it and determined to know why. She was afraid of something.

Peter asked her to stay with us, explaining that she would doubtless be helpful. He then questioned Mrs. Curtis and myself. We really had nothing to offer except the time we heard the scream. I remembered because I had looked at the clock thinking that I should be in Charlie's office. Grover, Charlie and Herbert had nothing to tell, because they came after we did. Peter excused them. They started away and looked inquiringly at me. I was too interested and didn't want to leave. If their curiosity was dead, mine wasn't. As Charlie left he whispered, "Invite that girl to dinner; me, too."

That was a presumption on Charlie's part and he knew it. I've always been a stickler about my dining-room. To me it is my holy of holies next to my bedroom. Just as there are people I wouldn't think of sleeping with, so are there people I refuse to dine with if I can help it, and I most certainly can in my own home.

He must have seen something flicker in my eyes. "Please," he coaxed and was gone. I gave him no sign and I never told him that I intended to do it, anyhow. If a man thinks he has planned or engineered a thing a woman is a fool to disillusion him. They get little enough out of life as it is, when you stop to think of it. Few women do. I've heard women say, "Oh, I wish I were a man!" That's sheer ignorance. Did you ever stop to think of a man's lot in life? He sees some pretty chit of a girl who decides that he will make her a good husband. From that moment until the day he dies the man doesn't have a chance. He asks the girl to marry him after she has encouraged him enough and then he keeps his nose to the grindstone for the rest of his life so that she can have the things she wants. I don't wonder some of them kick over the traces. There are exceptions to my observations, I know. I've seen women sacrifice their lives for their husbands and wondered why they were such fools, since the shoe is expected to be on the other foot.

Peter went to the door and gave his henchman there two orders. He was to find the bag of jewels in Mrs. Briggs' office and to bring the man Clayton with him when he returned. Peter then turned to Banter and asked,

"Did you see Mrs. Briggs this morning?"

"No. But I did talk to her on the telephone," Banter replied.

"At what time?"

"About a quarter of nine. I'm not sure; it was before the store opened."

"The time's right," Kramer interrupted. "Briggs called me in about the bag of jewelry. I was there when she asked Mr. Banter for an extra clerk."

"Why wasn't the Sutton girl discharged ?" Peter asked Kramer.

Banter broke in. "After all, we had no conclusive proof that the girl was a thief. Kramer has been watching her and hasn't been able to get a thing on her. We're short-handed on a day like this."

Peter turned to Kramer. "I want to talk to that girl. Bring her in here, will you? What's her job?"

"Sort of second assistant," Kramer replied.

"Okay. I won't keep you away from your store work any longer." Peter dismissed them both.

I was glad to see them go. Banter was all right, a little on the servile side, not a Uriah Heep exactly, but a distant relation. Kramer was the obnoxious one. I disliked them both.

While Peter was waiting for the man Clayton to be brought in he said, "This is slow, tiresome work, Miss Thomas."

I agreed that it was.

He surprised me by asking, "Do you think this crime was planned?"

"Murderers haven't been my line," I answered. I didn't know what he was driving at.

He laughed and said, "It's a pity. You'd have made a good detective. I've been watching your eyes. You've been doing a good bit of thinking while I've been asking questions and listening to answers."

"Was it planned?" I asked. He certainly gave me an opening.

"I don't think so," he replied thoughtfully. "It is what I call a spontaneous crime. That's why there are no clues except possibly the poison, which one of my men is working on now. The murderer thought fast, Miss Thomas. For some reason he wanted to be rid of Mrs. Briggs. He was given the incentive to kill first and the ready means of accomplishing it. Whether she died directly from strangulation or not doesn't matter. The murderer wanted it to look like suicide. Why?"

It seemed an obvious question to me, but before I had a chance to reply, Clayton was brought in by Smith the policeman, who reported that he was unable to find the bag of jewelry. Peter made no comment, but I was dying to know where the jewels were.

Clayton's section in the book department is right opposite the door in the partition. Peter asked him about the people who had used the door during the morning.

Clayton remembered Beth, Miss Blake the stationery buyer, John Carol and Eva Sutton of the jewelry department, also the electrician. When asked if there was any other means of entering the offices, he opened up a whole new series of possibilities for me. There was the door to which I had directed my Mrs. Kelly whose name I later discovered was Doyle. I may just as well call her by her right name now.

It was Clayton who called my attention to the other door in the little office directly opposite the one by which we had entered. I gasped then as I realized what it meant to any one investigating the crime. Peter laughed at me. "I take it back," he said.

"Take what back?" I asked, knowing full well what he meant.

"You should have noticed the extra doors," he said, mocking me.

"What do you know about them?" I asked.

"Each of these offices opens onto a rear corridor which runs parallel to the show windows on the side street. The show windows are used for furniture displays and the rear corridor is a wide one. The wide corridor connects with the elevators for the receiving-room."

"Anything else?" I asked. I knew he was pulling my leg, but I thought I would get as much information out of him as I could.

"That's all for the moment," he replied. There was an amused smile in his eyes as he said it.

"Do you mean to say you're wasting your time with all these questions when the murderer probably entered and left by that rear corridor?" I asked indignantly.

"Everything is under control," he assured me cockily.

He was so sure of himself that what followed was a terrible blow to him, I know, though for the life of me I don't see what he could have done about it.

Peter had been busy before I was called into the office. He is a smart young man and can't reasonably be blamed for what happened. I didn't know this at the time, but it belongs here. As soon as Peter arrived on the scene of the crime he investigated all entrances and exits and made inquiries about all doors and where they led. He sent a man out to the receiving-room at once to get the names of all the people who had entered the wide corridor from the receiving-room. William Evans, known in the store as Willie, was not at his post. He was out to his lunch. I know it sounds ridiculous, but they do crazy things in department stores. It seems that Willie was a checker as well as receiving clerk in the morning. He went on duty at six and I suppose he did want something to eat about ten. At any rate, he had gone when Peter sent his man for information. The man who was relieving Willie (I can't bear the name Willie and I imagine any man who is called it must deserve it) promised to notify the officer the moment Willie came back. That's why Peter was so cocksure. He expected to get the information he wanted.

In the meantime the man Clayton stood shifting from one foot to the other like an impatient crane. He was greatly relieved when Peter turned back to him and asked, "Did you notice anything unusual about any of the people who passed you going through that door?"

"No—" Clayton started, then stopped himself.

"Then you did?" Peter was eagerly alive.

"Well," Clayton hesitated, "when Miss Oliver came out she looked about as mad as a wet hen."

Peter didn't turn to look at Beth, but I did. She smiled at Clayton's remark as if she were secretly amused with herself.

"And," Clayton continued, "Miss Sutton had been crying, but," he hastened to add, "that wasn't unusual. Mrs. Briggs did get under people's skin. I spoke to her when she came back and she snapped at me. She was boiling mad."

"As soon as you heard Miss Oliver's scream you ran in here?" Peter asked.

"Yes."

"Did Miss Oliver scream immediately after she entered these offices?"

Clayton was puzzled by the question. He looked helplessly toward Beth, who helped him by saying, "He didn't see me enter."

"Then you came down the back elevators?"

"Yes," Beth replied.

"I wish you'd told me that before. That's all, Clayton."

As Clayton made his exit, Peter faced Beth. "Why were you angry when you went through the department?"

"It has nothing to do with the murder, really," she said quietly.

"Was it something Mrs. Briggs said or did?"

"No," she admitted reluctantly.

"Let me see—" Peter pretended to be thoughtful, but he wasn't. He was doing it to save Beth's feelings. "You said Mrs. Briggs' son was in the office with her. Did he do something to make you angry?"

"He accused me of spying," she retorted, and for a fraction of a moment her eyes snapped fire. I knew what Clayton meant when he said she looked as mad as a wet hen. I decided then and there that she had a temper and I was glad of it. I can't stand wishy-washy people.

"Because of the jewels?" he asked.

"Oh, no," she answered quickly. "It's really a personal thing, Mr. Conklin, and just a little distasteful."

"I'm sorry, Miss Oliver, but I can't pass even a seemingly unimportant detail in a case of this kind. If it has no bearing on the case, I'll forget it immediately."

"Would you like me to go?" I bent forward and asked.

"I'd rather you stayed," she said with feeling. I knew then that I was giving her moral support. She turned from me to Peter, squared herself and told the story.

"Carl Briggs—" she began, and stopped. I could see the pulse in her throat quiver. Poor dear, what she had to say was not going to be easy. Peter was patient. I suppose he sensed some revelation which would have definite bearing on the case. He didn't urge her. She was for all the world like some one about to plunge into the cold surf.

"Carl Briggs is my husband," she said, and without waiting or paying any attention to my gasp of surprise or Peter's rather satisfied smile hurried on. "We've been married several months and lived together until last night, when I definitely left him."

"Why?" Peter asked.

"I'm sure it has nothing to do with Mrs. Briggs'

death," she evaded.

"But you did go to see your husband this morning after you learned that Mrs. Briggs had been murdered, didn't you?" Peter insisted.

"Yes," she replied softly.

"Why?"

"Is it true, Mr. Conklin, that a wife cannot be made to testify against her husband?" Beth asked.

"This isn't a court of law, Miss Oliver," he replied.

"But you are looking for a suspect. You have sent for Carl. You would like to fasten the guilt on him and give yourself a case," she reasoned.

"I'm not anxious for a case against any person unless that person happens to be guilty," he replied fairly enough. "You must realize that your present attitude leads me to believe that you suspect your husband yourself."

"But I don't!" she protested quickly. "Circumstances seem to be against him, that is all. You know he was in the office this morning."

"Did Mrs. Briggs know that you had broken with her son?" he asked.

"I told her last night," Beth answered.

"What did she say?"

"She was annoyed with me. She had been very pleased with our marriage."

"Why did you suddenly decide to drop Carl Briggs?" Peter asked, rather cleverly I thought. One way or another he was going to get the story out of Beth.

"It wasn't sudden." There was a heavy overtone in her voice.

"Just why did you sever your relations with Briggs?" Peter asked. I was wondering why she married the man at all. I knew nothing about him, but somehow it struck me as having been a misalliance from the very start.

"Mr. Briggs," she replied, "is what is commonly known as a ladies' man. And not too particular," she added. "I happened to overhear some of the girls talking in the washroom yesterday. They were talking about me, Mr. Briggs and some of the other girls in the department."

"And you didn't like the things you heard?" Peter suggested.

"I did not."

"What did you do about it?"

"I told Mrs. Briggs last night that I was through with Carl."

"This conversation you overheard. Was it so terrible?" he asked.

"It was cheap and vulgar."

I knew exactly what she meant. I've heard parts of weird conversations in washrooms, things revolting to a sensitive person.

"You explained your feelings to Mrs. Briggs?" Peter went on.

"Yes."

"Did you have to explain the details?"

"Mrs. Briggs never dealt in half-measures," she said, giving me another facet to the Briggs woman's character.

"So that was why Briggs accused you of spying?"

"Undoubtedly. I've noticed that mothers are willing to sacrifice anything and anybody for their sons." That was an observation which surprised me. She was a little young to have been so accurately aware of the fact. She went on, "Mrs. Briggs considered me a good influence in Carl's life. She wanted to keep us together. She was furious with me last night because I refused to change my mind. Mrs. Briggs had a temper and I rather suspect she upbraided Carl this morning about his attentions to girls in the department."

"But," Peter objected, "you were in her department. Why did she encourage you?"

The point was well taken and I waited for Beth's answer.

"I was her assistant, not just a clerk, and I think," she hesitated just a moment, "she respected me."

"The conversation you overheard. Was it about some

particular girl?" he asked.

"Must I answer that?" she begged.

"No, but it would help if you would. I'm not trying to pry into people's lives, you know. I'm looking for the motive to a murder."

"But why would Eva Sutton want to kill her?" Beth asked. "She didn't know anything about the conversation or my stand in the matter."

I don't know that Beth mentioned the girl's name intentionally. It was a natural defensive statement and at the moment Peter took no notice of it.

"Why did you go to see your husband this morning?" Peter returned to that phase of the questioning. "Did you want to warn him?"

"In his way he was fond of his mother. I wanted to be able to tell him myself. I thought under the circumstances it was the least I could do."

"How did he take it?" Peter asked.

"He wasn't there."

That, I think, stumped Peter a little. It certainly was flat after the excitement I, at least, was feeling.

"Thank you," Peter said. "Now, one thing more before you go. When you came down in the receiving-room elevator, did you see any one coming out of the corridor?"

"No."

"Did you hear any one or anything?"

"No. I was rather intent on getting on the floor. Mrs. Briggs depended on me to look after things. I should be out there now, if you are through with me." She stood up, her attitude asking permission to go on with her work.

"You may go," Peter said, "but I'd like you to be ready if I need you again."

Beth left her hat and coat on the clothes-tree in the corner of the office. After she had gone and we heard the door in the outer partition close, Peter turned to me and said, "Why doesn't she tell all she knows?"

So Peter had the same feeling about her that I had!

"An unwilling witness," he went on, "is one of our

greatest problems."

"It seems to me she has told you plenty," I retorted.

"Women always side with each other, don't they?"

I knew he was teasing, but I answered, "We have to."

Peter next questioned Miss Blake, the stationery buyer, who said she and her assistant had been on the floor from eight o'clock on and knew nothing about the murder.

Peterson, the doorman, was a blank. He had been so busy, he said, watching the people coming into the store that he had not noticed the little door at all.

I suppose I should have mentioned the Irish woman, Mrs. Doyle, then; but I didn't, because she didn't seem to be important at the time. A woman with a falling petticoat and a broken garter is much too busy to be thinking of murder. I know and I've never had the misfortune to break both of them at once.

John Carol, the clerk from the jewelry department, was questioned next.

"You were in here this morning?" Peter asked.

"Yes, sir."

"At what time?"

"I don't know exactly, but it was before nine."

"Why did you come in?"

"I answered the buzzer," Carol replied with a sheepish grin. Peter smiled too, but I didn't understand the allusion.

"You mean the new one?" Peter asked.

"Yes, sir. Just after the electrician came out to tell us that it was installed, it rang insistently. I answered it."

"What did Mrs. Briggs want?"

"Eva Sutton."

"Was Mrs. Briggs alone?"

"No, sir. Her son was with her."

Peter looked at the top of the partition as he said, "These partitions are not very high. Did you happen to hear any of their conversation as you came in or went out?"

Carol's eyes went to the top of the partition before he answered, "I did hear them."

"What were they saying?"

This digging and delving into the privacy of people seemed distasteful to me, but I realized that Peter could get nowhere unless he amassed information.

"It was Mr. Briggs. He was mad. I picked up part of a sentence. I heard him say, '—and I'm telling you to mind your own business. I'm going to get the money and I'm not going to let you stand in my way.' I coughed then," Carol said, "to warn them I was there. When I entered the office Mr. Briggs had stopped talking, but his face was red. Mrs. Briggs told me what she wanted and I left immediately."

"Hear anything else?"

"No, sir."

"All right, Carol, thanks. You may go."

Carol was glad to get away.

Eva Sutton came in next. She was a blonde, fairly natural too. I'm an authority on blondes. I was one myself until my hair became so thin that I had to get the transformation which I now wear. She was a rather pathetic creature, with sad, pale-blue eyes. She had very smooth fair skin, but used too much liquid powder. She wasn't the hard cold type of blonde that you so often see; she seemed rather beaten to me, as if life had demanded too much from her. She was shortish and thin to the point of emaciation. She needed food, good food, but I suppose she was like all the modern young women who try their best, even going so far as ruining their health, to look like slats. I've seen women do a lot of crazy things in the course of my life, but I think the elimination of curves and the gradual evolution to flat chests, is one of the most unfeminine things they have ever done. They talk about allure, meaning gaunt faces and slim figures. I'll bet you right now if you were to ask ten men which they would prefer, nine of them would vote for hips and bosoms, and all your skinny allure would be thrown overboard, as it ought to be. These wind-blown walking poles you see on the avenue now have just about as much feminine allure as a green lamppost. Take ten married men who have skinny wives and a mistress on the side and you'll find the mistress is built as a woman should be. There's nothing comforting about a skinny woman. Did you ever hear of any one weeping comfortably on a flat chest?

Eva Sutton was nervous as she stood before Peter.

"Sit down," he suggested.

She slid into a chair gratefully. She tried to be composed, but I noticed her hands flutter. Her nails were dyed that terrible deep red. I dare say her toe-nails were, too. She looked like that.

Peter Conklin had an interesting technique. In the first place, he didn't look like a policeman and he didn't sound like one. He asked Eva Sutton several seemingly unimportant questions, which she answered readily enough when she realized he wasn't going to bite her. She became a little more at ease after we had learned that she was a second assistant and was responsible for the department when Mrs. Briggs or Beth Oliver was not in evidence.

"You were probably the last person to see Mrs. Briggs alive," Peter said. "Tell me about it, will you, please?"

"There isn't very much to tell. She sent for me and gave me one of her usual lectures right in front of her son," she answered bitterly.

"About her son?" Peter's question was innocence itself.

The Sutton girl flushed and her eyes flashed fear for a moment.

"Did she say that?" she asked.

"Mrs. Briggs?" Peter asked in turn.

"How could she if she was dead? I mean Oliver."

A woman could read a lot into that statement of hers. There was resentment of Beth in that speech and something more, jealousy tinged with fear perhaps.

"How would Miss Oliver know?" he countered.

"Oliver told her about Carl and me, that's why," she

retorted.

"Then Mrs. Briggs did scold you about her son right in front of him, too?" Peter seemed surprised.

"No," the girl replied quickly.

"Then why did she scold you? You were crying when you went back to the department."

"She gave me a bag of jewelry which Oliver says she found in the stockroom. Mrs. Briggs didn't say I stole the darned stuff, but she made some wide-open hints I'm no fool. I know what she was driving at. All the stuff in that bag came from my section, but I didn't know anything about it. Honest I didn't."

"Did you know about the shortages in the jewelry department?"

"Say, you couldn't work in this store and not know about it," she answered.

"Have you any idea about the jewels? Some one must have taken them up there, intending to dispose of them," he suggested.

"I have ideas, yes," she admitted, "but I'm not going to say anything. I don't want to get in trouble."

"What sort of trouble?" he asked.

"Mrs. Briggs is dead, isn't she?" the girl replied.

"Then you think the store thefts have something to do with her death?"

"I won't answer you," she cried. "I won't! You can't make me! I need my job. I can't afford to be out of work, and I don't know anything anyhow!" She was hysterical by the time she had finished.

"All right, Miss Sutton. Don't get yourself into a state," he said kindly. "We'll forget about the jewels, for the time being."

She calmed down after that and didn't see the significance of his next question as I did.

"When was the last time you saw Carl Briggs, privately I mean?"

"A couple of days ago," she replied.

"You are quite sure, Miss Sutton?" he urged.

"I ought to know when I saw him," she flashed back, the color in her cheeks rising.

"How did you know that Miss Oliver told Mrs. Briggs about you and her son?"

"He told me," she replied.

"When?"

"The other night when I saw him," she answered readily enough. I knew the poor thing was trapped and felt sorry for her.

"That's very strange." Peter shook his head thoughtfully.

The girl was uncomfortable. She began to squirm. I once saw a rat caught in a wire trap and she reminded me of it. She knew she was caught and she wanted to extricate herself, but she didn't know how to do it.

"I can't understand it," Peter continued after a moment. He looked straight at the girl then and spoke slowly. "Miss Oliver didn't know until yesterday that you were interested in Mr. Briggs."

"Huh!" It was a polite way of suggesting that Beth was a liar. Why do women fight so with each other over men? Heavens! They're like street-cars. There's always another one along in a minute or so.

"You seem doubtful," he suggested.

"She's known about me for a long time," she replied with an air of swagger.

"Mrs. Briggs?" Peter asked.

"No. Oliver. She tried to break it up. We were just friends. We've known each other for a long time." She seemed a bit hasty in her explanation. "She was jealous," she added.

"If you haven't seen Mr. Briggs privately for several days, how could he have told you what he did when he didn't know it himself until he came to see his mother this morning?"

"I don't know," she answered helplessly.

"Why don't you tell me the truth?" he suggested. "It can't harm any one."

She remained stolid and silent.

"You don't want Mr. Briggs to get into trouble, do you?" he asked.

"No." It was only one word, but it was freighted with feeling.

"You're not helping him by your silence. As a matter of fact, you've made me very curious. I work on the theory that you don't try to hide things unless there is something to hide."

"He didn't do it. He couldn't have done it. He was with me. He left me just a minute or so before the scream came," she defended.

"And where were you?"

"We were out by the receiving-room elevators," she replied. "Willie can tell you that."

"I'll check that point with Willie when I see him," he assured her. "Since you know he didn't do it, I don't see why you were so reluctant to tell me about having seen him."

"He told me not to say anything about it," she answered without thinking.

"When?" Peter's tone was careless. I leaned forward. Were we going to get the answer to the riddle so easily?

"When I telephoned him," she answered.

"You called him to tell him she had committed suicide, was that it?"

"No. To tell him she was murdered."

"How did you know?"

I wondered about that, too, and waited eagerly for her answer.

"Clayton." She went on to explain. "He had his ear glued to that partition from the time the body was found. When they discovered it was murder and not suicide, Clayton came over and told us. It was then I telephoned Carl. He said, 'Better not say anything about seeing me. You know what the police are.' He didn't do it, mister. Honest he didn't."

"By telling me you have given him an alibi," he

assured her. "Tell me something else. Did you see any one go into the wide corridor while you were talking to Mr. Briggs?"

She considered for a moment before she spoke. "Only Oliver. When she stepped off the elevator we kept out of sight. I talked to Carl for a few minutes more before he left. Then I stopped to speak to Willie and was just coming back into the department when I heard the scream."

"Were you returning by way of the corridor?" he asked.

"No. There's a door into the store from the receiving-room."

"How long was it from the time you saw Miss Oliver until you heard the scream?"

"It might have been ten minutes; I don't know."

"And you saw no one enter or leave the corridor while you were there?" He repeated the question.

"No one but Oliver." She was positive of that point.

"That's all, Miss Sutton."

She started away, but he stopped her. "Was Mr. Briggs with his mother when you left her office?"

She did some mental calculating before she answered his question rather reluctantly. "Yes," she said.

"Any idea of the time?"

"Quarter of nine, I guess. I dunno."

"You may go."

The girl left hurriedly, glad to get away. I didn't like her, but I did feel sorry for the poor thing. She knew Briggs was going to be involved and she had tried to help him by making things look bad for Beth Oliver.

"It makes it look bad for Miss Oliver, doesn't it?" Peter asked.

"Now you're talking like a policeman," I retorted, "and you know it. What about the son?"

"They're in it together," he said. "There's more to this than meets the eye."

"Bosh!" I exploded. "So far you haven't a thing against

the Oliver girl except your unfounded suspicions and the testimony of that blonde baggage who was just in here."

"Then why doesn't the Oliver girl talk? What is she holding back?" he demanded.

I couldn't answer that question, because I didn't know.

# CHAPTER SIX

Richard Davis, Peter's secretary, or rather I should say stenographer (Peter says detectives don't have secretaries, it sounds too sissy), had been a very busy young man up to the time Eva Sutton left the little office. I had my first good look at him when he raised his head from that pad over which he had been so intent. He had a wide face, clear, rather large blue eyes and a crop of short stubby hair one shade removed from blond—you know, the in-between color. German origin, I decided. He smiled, which rather surprised me. He had seemed so serious, but I don't suppose you have time for anything else if you have to sit and make those funny little crisscross marks on paper as people talk. For the life of me, I don't see how he can read them back as glibly as he does. Those notes which he can read so easily have been of great help to me in the writing of this book. Even now, months after it all happened, he can turn to any particular spot I mention with uncanny accuracy and read just what I want to know. I suppose his shorthand training stands him in good stead now, otherwise he would never be able to read my deplorable scrawl. My cacography is supposed to be full of character, which is utter nonsense. It's so bad I very often can't read what I've written myself, once the ink is dry.

Davis dug into his pocket and pulled out a package of cigarettes and said with a nod toward me, "Do you mind?"

Mind! Heavens above! I reached for one of them avidly. There are times when I think chivalry has been dead for centuries, due largely to the thoughtlessness of women; and then Charlie says or does a nice thing or a man like Davis shows the deference and consideration which I was brought up to expect and I readjust my ideas until some flagrant discourtesy infuriates me all over again.

"Like to stretch your legs and rest your hand?" Peter asked.

Davis gave him a warm appreciative smile and stood up.

"You have the Oliver girl's address," Peter said. "Send a man up there to see what he can find. Knickknacks would be interesting, if any," he suggested. "And while you're at it, send some one around to the Sutton girl's apartment on the same mission. Also remind Smith that I'm waiting for the Briggs man. He doesn't live more than four blocks from here and could have crawled over by this time."

With Davis out of the way I said to Peter, "I've enjoyed this. Thanks for letting me stay."

"You'll soon get tired of it. You've seen how routine it is when you get right down to it," he said matter-of-factly.

It may be routine to Peter, but the glimpses into people's lives I had had whetted my curiosity for more. "Are you really serious about the Oliver girl?" I asked him point-blank.

"She's holding out on me and that's something a detective doesn't take lightly."

"Rot."

"Rot or not," he came back defensively, his eyes gleaming, "this woman wasn't murdered for fun, you know. The Oliver girl knew the woman rather intimately. She was married to the son. Do you suppose she broke with him just because of what she happened to hear in the washroom?"

"Of course she did," I replied. "That girl is not cheap. She looks and acts as if she has been well bred. If we knew more of the conversation she overheard we might understand her better. You have some imagination, haven't you?"

He laughed. I like people to laugh when I get caustic. I've grown to expect it.

"There's this thieving to be taken into consideration,

too," he went on after a moment. "The Oliver girl knew about the shortages. She says she found the bag of jewels in the stockroom."

"Don't you believe her?" I asked.

"Not too much," he replied thoughtfully.

"That girl is honest, no matter what else she may be," I insisted.

"I can't go on a woman's intuition," he grinned impishly. "I must get at the facts."

"You've allowed the Sutton girl to influence your judgment," I accused.

"Perhaps. The Sutton girl is and probably has been jealous of this Lothario son of the murdered woman for whom we are waiting and her testimony isn't too trustworthy, for that reason. While she didn't exactly accuse the Oliver girl of stealing, you were left to draw your own conclusions from what she said. Now, I know what you're going to say," he stopped me before I could even begin. "The Sutton girl is holding back, too, and I'm going to get to the bottom of this before I'm through. I have to find the murderer and to do so I must know why the murder was committed."

The store was a mad-house of mystery, evidently. My reason for being there at all was because they didn't really know why business was so bad. Unless the woman was murdered for personal reasons, her death must have had something to do with the store. Would the amount of jewelry, silver, etc., stolen provide a sufficient motive? Of one thing I was positive—the Oliver girl was neither a thief nor a murderess. I've always been interested in men because they offer more variety, but this girl captured my imagination. She was so lovely. I don't mean pretty. I haven't much use for pretty women. You see, I was one of seven girls and they were all beautiful except me. If you have been reared with a bevy of beauties you may understand a little of my feeling on the subject of pretty women and appreciate perhaps the agonies I suffered as a growing girl until I realized that there were other things attractive to men and some women outside of beauty.

I knew a charming woman years ago—a fine woman, too. At the first glance she was positively ugly; that is, as far as facial features were concerned. She had a largish, slightly pitted nose, rough skin and a mouth that was all wrong, but after you had been in her company for ten minutes you didn't think about her looks. Her eyes were bright and alive. She was one of the few people I've known who really had charm. She had a soothing voice and she was cramfull of ideas. She had so much to give and did it graciously. She was an excellent talker, but a far better listener and had the knack of making you talk. When you left her you were rather drunk at the sound of your own voice, only you didn't know it. You thought she was a brilliant conversationalist. She was, if and when you gave her a chance.

Beth wasn't like that. She was lovely to look at and I felt she was fine. I've heard men say that some women are the salt of the earth and they didn't mean beauty. They meant a woman who had the qualities which have made the world go round. I could see Beth as a wife and mother. Not one of these sentimentalized Mother's Day mothers, but a woman who would live, work for and understand her family without any thought for herself except the satisfaction she derived from the service rendered.

I've lived long enough to know that one of the greatest mistakes we make in our contacts with people is giving them the qualities, in our own imagination, that we would like them to have. I didn't want to be wrong about Beth. Perhaps my intuition was at work. Charlie liked her and I wanted her to like me. If she didn't, it would mean the end of my friendship with him. I'm no fool. I know what a woman can do with a man. I've seen long friendships end with a sudden pop because of women.

I looked at Peter intently for a moment and said, "Do you want to make a bet?"

"Depends," he hedged.

"I'll bet you anything you like, the Oliver girl is innocent of even the slightest connection with the case except for the misfortune of having been the first to find the body."

"You're on," he agreed. "Ten dollars against a new hat."

"For me or for you?" I asked.

"What?"

"The hat. Mine cost much more than ten dollars," I warned.

"If you win you get ten dollars. If I win you buy me a hat. Agreed?" he asked.

"Agreed," I replied, "if you will let me continue to be in on your investigation."

"If you get any kick out of it, it's okay with me. I don't see why you are so interested. It's so long-winded. We're always hoping a hot tip may be just round the corner. If it isn't, we have to wait." He went to the door and called petulantly to Smith, "Hasn't that Willie man returned to duty yet?"

"You seem to think he's important," I said, hoping to get his reasons.

"Of course he is. If none of the people who went through the door into the department are guilty, then the murderer probably came in the rear way and either left by that entrance or through the little door which our friend Peterson, unfortunately for us, was not watching. Yes, ma'am. Willie ought to give us some good suspects." He was thinking out-loud when he made the last remark and not talking to me.

I had an idea and asked, "When do you think the murder was committed?"

"I can't tell until after I've checked with this Willie person and Mrs. Briggs' son. Damn him, anyhow! I hope he isn't making a getaway. He was warned early enough."

"That would be evidence of guilt?" I asked.

"Well, it would be highly suspicious," he admitted.

"Would it help to remind you that the scream came at

exactly ten minutes past nine by the store clock?"

"It's a good thing to know," he answered appreciatively.

I went on. "It was about eight-thirty when the electrician finished his work. Shortly after that Carol came in here. Then the Sutton girl followed. You didn't ask her how long she stayed," I accused.

"Checking back on me, eh? She said about a quarter of nine," he grinned. "The son was the last person we know to see her alive. When I question him I'll have a fairly accurate idea of the time when the murder was committed."

"If the son didn't do it," I said, "she was probably killed between five minutes of nine o'clock and a minute or two after."

"Getting it down pretty fine, aren't you?" he asked. This time he didn't grin.

"It couldn't have been more than a minute or two after nine when the Oliver girl arrived at the office," I continued.

"Why?"

"Because she started down after she heard the opening bell and was seen by Briggs and Miss Sutton. The Sutton girl went back to the department and Miss Oliver came into the office and discovered the body."

"Which, according to your own statement, gave the Oliver girl at least five minutes to kill the woman and prepare the suicide set-up," he said glibly, and I could have slapped him and bitten my tongue at the same time. I do talk too much, there is no question about that.

"Miss Oliver was doing her work at the same time, trying to make noise enough to rouse the woman out of what she supposed was a cat-nap," I retorted, trying to patch up the blunder I had made.

"That's what you think," he taunted me annoyingly.

I hadn't given up the idea which had prompted me to determine the time of the murder. I stood up. "I'm going out into the store," I explained.

"What for?" he asked.

"Looking for clues. If anything happens while I'm away, will you have your young man read it to me? I .want to be completely posted."

He agreed.

I went in search of Beth Oliver. Poor dear, there were purple shadows under her eyes. She managed a smile when I approached her. "Could you do me a favor?" I asked.

"Gladly," she replied at once. She wasn't just being nice to a customer or an old lady, either.

"Get the Sandy McLeod person for me, will you? I have a job I want him to do for me," I offered in explanation.

She turned to a telephone and asked the operator to locate Sandy and send him to the jewelry department.

"He'll be here in a few minutes," she said as she replaced the telephone.

"Will you have dinner with me some night soon, to-night or to-morrow?" I made it definite because I can't abide people who say, "Come up and see me some time," and that includes the imitators of Mae West past and present. It was a sudden invitation, but that didn't bother her.

"I'd like to very much," she accepted graciously. "I'd prefer to come to-morrow."

"To-morrow it is, then. I'll probably have a man or two just to liven us up," I said. I noticed a flicker in her eyes and knew she was thinking about clothes. "It will be quite informal. Would you care to come directly from the store or would you prefer to go home first? I dine at seven-thirty usually, but it's flexible."

"Seven-thirty will give me time to go home," she said just as Sandy approached.

I took that red-faced, rather surprised young man by the arm, marched him down the aisle and told him what I wanted. "She's plumpish, has a good red face, unmistakably Irish, with straggly hair, wears a worn blue coat tight under the arms and her skirt is not more than three inches from the floor."

"Those are things only a woman would notice," he said appreciatively. "What'll I say to her? How'll I know she's the right one? There might be two of them."

"Ask her if she's the woman who broke her garter getting into the store this morning," I instructed.

"And probably get a slap in the face," he said dolefully,

"Be tactful," I advised; "and bring her to me in the book department."

"But what reason will I give her?" he insisted.

"Tell her the rosary she bought," I started, and stopped, because I was afraid I might be treading on dangerous ground. "Tell her anything. Accuse her of shoplifting. I don't care, so long as you bring her to me in the book department where I'll be waiting—and hurry," I urged. "It's important."

They have an efficient system in department stores. He went to a telephone, gave a description of the woman to the operator, and in a few minutes I heard the bonging signals sounding all over the place.

I went back to Beth, borrowed a pencil from her and printed my address on the back of my card and gave it to her. Then I went to the book department to wait. A clerk tried to interest me in some of the latest novels, but I couldn't concentrate. My mind was on the Irish woman, Mrs. Doyle. I was staking a lot on her.

My mind had been so full of murder all morning that I had quite forgotten my reason for being in the store at all on a Sales Day. I went back to Beth and asked her to get Charlie Doane on the telephone for me. I explained to Charlie that I was too interested in the pursuit of the murderer to waste time on a meeting. I did ask him if he could postpone it until late afternoon and, lamb that he is, he agreed. We made it tentatively for sometime after five-thirty. After he had set the time he asked me quite solicitously if I would be too tired. He suggested taking time off for lunch and a rest. I had no patience with that idea. I never rest in the daytime. Beds were made for use at night. I like to be doing things all day, old as I am. My doctor says I have the vitality of a horse when in reality I ought to be done up in lavender and lace and a poke-bonnet, resting and dozing in the shade of my boudoir. When I reach the lavender and lace period I hope I die, because I'll be of no use to myself and nothing but a nuisance to my servants and friends.

"I'm not going to eat lunch and perhaps miss something really interesting," I retorted. I heard him chuckle and hang up.

I went back to Beth. I wanted to know something about the girl. I talk a lot about family and all that sort of thing, when, as a matter of fact, I like people for what they are themselves and not because of their ancestors. I've known well-bred bores and scamps—more bores than scamps, as I think about it. Family background can't make a person, but it does give a frame if they have anything in themselves, though all it does for most of them is to make them snobbishly insufferable. I've heard a lot of family talk since the depression from people who are living in the glories of the past and trying to keep their social prestige up in their reduced circumstances instead of making the best of what they have. Less talk and some of the grit which their hardy ancestors had would do a lot for them financially. Beth, at least, was working. I'm sure she could have found an easier way. Since we had no common ground I wanted to find something from which we could build, so I asked very bluntly,

"Was your grandfather, or father, for that matter, Stephen Oliver?"

She was clearly surprised as she answered, "Yes, my grandfather."

"Then you were educated abroad?" I felt positive, but I wanted to be sure.

"In a convent in France," she replied.

"I knew your grandfather," I explained, quite satisfied with myself. Old Stephen Oliver might have been a foolish man about town, but he had family, traditions and breeding, and even the chorus girl grandmother of Beth hadn't hurt her any. As a matter of fact, the girl before me probably owed a great deal to that grandmother. I've noticed so-called blue blood running pretty thin these days after too much fine breeding. When I look at some of the children of our present first families I shudder a little. They are so thin, pale and puny. A dose of good healthy common blood would buck up the lot of them. At least, it would make them more alive and less dull.

"He died last year," she said.

"He was an old man," I answered, thinking back. "He must have been about seventy-one or two. He was a little younger than I. We often danced together."

She made no reply to that. There is nothing to say to an old person's reminiscences except, "Is that so?" or, "How nice!" and I hate the people who do it.

"Do you realize," I asked point-blank, "that the detective is inclined to suspect you?"

She flushed and answered, "I had that feeling."

I did a thing then for which there is no excuse. It wasn't fair to Peter, but I said, "He is wondering what you did from the time you entered her office until you screamed. He says you must have been in there for at least five minutes."

"I was," she replied with disarming candor.

"Well," I advised, "you'd better have a good story ready for him. He'll be after you again unless he finds something better."

She stepped out into the aisle between two counters and came close to my side. Her voice was low as she began, "I don't mean to be presumptuous, Miss Thomas, but I don't know what to do. Are you financially interested in the store?"

Her question did surprise me and before answering I used the old trick of asking a question myself. "Why do you ask that?"

"I couldn't tell you my reason unless you were. I thought that perhaps you were a stockholder."

"It isn't generally known," I finally decided to tell her, "but between us Charles Doane and I control the stock. Now what is on your mind?"

"I can't tell you here or now. To-morrow night at dinner, if you won't have any one else, I'll tell you then."

"Is there any reason why you can't come to-night?" I asked. I didn't want to wait a whole day for the thing she was going to tell me. Imagine waiting twenty-four hours or longer for information! Why, the curiosity would just about ruin me.

"We'll have to work late to-night, clearing up after the sale," she explained.

"Bother the work!" I said. "Come to dinner anyhow. Can't you let some one else do it for you?"

"You really don't know much about department stores, do you ?" she asked. "There's so much to be done, Miss Thomas, and without Mrs. Briggs the brunt of it will fall on me. If I were to shirk responsibility now, I might lose my position and the chance to become the buyer. It's very important that I have something to do. I must work," she explained, giving me a good understanding of her economic situation.

I was glad Peter didn't hear that speech. His police mind would probably have decided there and then that she killed the Briggs woman to get the job. I suppose such things have happened. According to the press, there are all sorts of reasons for murder.

"Well, it'll have to be to-morrow night, then, and we'll be alone," I agreed. Then I remembered Charlie's request. "If it's important, and I'm sure it is, perhaps we'd better have Mr. Doane with us," I suggested.

"If you think best," she agreed.

"This information you have for us?" I asked. "Is that what you were holding back when you talked to the detective?"

It startled her as I hoped it would. "I've already been forced to incriminate one person," she said, "which I didn't enjoy doing."

"You mean the Sutton girl?" I asked quickly. "You couldn't help yourself. Earlier this morning you were on the point of giving Carl Briggs' telephone number. Why didn't you do it?"

"I didn't think it wise," she answered. She seemed startled.

"Rubbish," I said impatiently. "What do you know about Briggs that you don't want to tell the police? You must realize that your silence makes things seem much blacker for you and for him." She didn't answer. She should have told me to mind my own business, but she didn't, so I went on. "Since they suspect you, to save your neck you'll have to tell it eventually, so why not now?"

"It seems unnecessarily mean to cast suspicion on another person," she replied; "and, besides, there's a more important reason."

"There are people who aren't considering you with that nicety," I warned. "You should tell."

"It may not be necessary," she evaded.

"Why not let me be the judge of that?" I asked.

"To-morrow night, then," she answered after a moment's consideration.

"You may be in jail," I said brutally.

That bothered her, as I meant it should. I did feel sorry for her, because I had made her afraid for herself and had her battling with that fear and her sense of decency.

"I'll have to take that risk," she replied with finality. I admired her for that speech. I like grit and fearlessness.

# CHAPTER SEVEN

I saw Sandy in the main aisle going toward the book department with Mrs. Doyle in tow. I hurried after them.

There were a number of things racing about in my mind. What did Beth Oliver want to tell me? What did she know about the son that she hadn't told? Did she think the son had killed his mother for her money? For a moment I doubted her. Perhaps she was just a smart shrewd woman looking for a wealthy husband. Had Charlie's attentions given her ideas? Was that her real reason for breaking with Briggs? Had she purposely worked on my curiosity with this important secret she had to tell me, so that I would ask Charlie to dinner with her? If that was her game I had certainly played into her hands. I've known some smart women in my day who could engineer things beautifully. I've done enough of it myself to recognize it while it's being done. If she wanted Charlie she didn't have to use me as a go-between. He was too obviously interested in her himself. No, the girl was genuine. I was letting my imagination run away with me.

Mrs. Doyle was waddling along beside Sandy like a broad boat in a heavy sea. There was something about the set of her body as her one free arm swung which made me feel that she wasn't doing it at all gladly. Sandy stopped at the book department and looked about just as I came up to them.

"Oh! It's you," she greeted me.

"Thank you, Sandy," I said, dismissing him. I told Mrs. Doyle my name. She reciprocated by telling me hers, which, of course, I knew.

"I was wondering who it was as knew I broke me garter," she said with a good-natured twinkle in her eye.

"I think you can probably do me and the store a great

favor," I started my explanation.

"How can the likes of me do you a favor?" she asked skeptically.

"I don't know," I answered truthfully enough. "I'm hoping you can. Do you remember the door I pointed out to you this morning?"

"Indeed and I do. And a haven of refuge it was."

"Something terrible has happened in the store, Mrs. Doyle. I'd like you to go with me to the detective and talk with him."

"Not on your life!" she refused immediately.

"Please," I urged.

"I don't want to be mixed up with the police," she said flatly.

"Mr. Charles Doane and myself are vitally interested in what has happened. We just hoped that you might have seen or heard something"

"You mean the man who owns the store?" she asked.

"Yes."

"Now, what could I know?" she grinned at me. "I don't even know what it is that happened."

"Didn't you hear the scream?" I asked, my hopes falling.

"You'd have to be deaf not to and me that close to the sound of it."

"It's about that. Won't you?"

"Well—"

"There'll be no complications for you," I assured her. "This may just be an old woman's whim. I'm turning detective."

"Are you, now?" She looked at me speculatively. "You don't look so old."

"Seventy-five," I said. I know I don't look it, but I like to see the incredulous doubt on people's faces when I tell them. Up to my sixty-fifth birthday I felt my age was nobody's business, but from that point on, knowing that I am remarkable for my age (I've seen so many museum pieces at seventy), I've been rather boastful. Why be remarkable if you can't get some fun out of it?

"Go 'way!'" Mrs. Doyle grinned and I rather anticipated a poke in the ribs, which didn't materialize.

"True," I assured her. "You're a young-looking woman yourself."

"Sixty," she replied proudly, "and nothing the matter with me much but varicose veins and a touch of blood-pressure now and then."

We were getting quite chummy. I was doing my best to make the woman like me. She gave me a glance which was more squint than anything else and said, "And what is it you're detectin'?"

"If you'll promise not to tell—" I leaned toward her and paused, "—murder."

"Glory be to God! Here! This morning!" she gasped.

I nodded.

"I'll have none of it!" She made me think of a great turtle crawling into its shell. Her refusal was so emphatic.

"Mrs. Kelly—" I started to plead.

"Doyle's the name," she reminded me snappishly.

"Mrs. Doyle. Surely you want a criminal brought to justice? The woman who was killed, a poor soul so fat she was unable to get around easily, was done to death in her office this morning." I was making no impression on her. She had made up her Irish mind. I had to do something. "Killed while she was praying, her rosary torn apart by her death struggles." I threw the words at her hopefully.

"God rest her soul," she muttered. "Saying her prayers, you say? The poor creature." She crossed herself.

"A good woman," I went on, "foully murdered. I want to find the fiend who did it. Imagine, it might have been one of us."

"I'd like to see any one try it!" she said belligerently.

"I hoped you might have seen or heard something," I went on, making my voice sound very hopeless.

"I don't know anything about it. How could I?"

"The detective has been unable to unearth any clues

so far," I explained. "I just thought that since you were in that little corridor you might have chanced to hear or see something which would be important."

"I was too busy fixing myself. Maybe you've never tried to fix a petticoat and a garter at the same time."

"If you would just talk to the detective," I urged. "They have ways of learning things, putting two and two together, as it were, that people like us would never think of. Little things which to us are unimportant become significant under their questioning."

"Don't I know it," she assured me. "You read about it in the papers all the time."

"Then you'll do it?"

At that moment I saw Peter's face appear at the door in the partition. "Please come," I urged. "I'll take you in there and tell the detective you'll talk to him."

"I suppose one good turn deserves another, but mind, now," she warned, "I don't want to be mixed up in nothing, and," she added, "it'll do no good."

In the little corridor we found Smith. I told him to find Mrs. Doyle a chair.

"I'll be glad to rest my feet if nothing else," she said. I wondered what she would say if she knew that Smith was leading her into the office where Mrs. Briggs had been killed. I went into the next room to see Peter. Davis was back at his desk with pencil ready.

I told Peter I had a witness for him.

"She'll have to wait. Briggs has just arrived. I thought you were going to miss it. Sit over there." He pointed to a chair.

"Anything new develop?" I asked.

"A report from the doctor. Her heart gave out at the shock. She probably died from fear of being strangled. The poison is a polish, mostly prussic acid, which they use to clean metals."

"Then it was planted to make it look like suicide?"

"Exactly. Did you get any information from the Oliver girl?" he asked with a grin.

"No." I was annoyed with him. Why did he think he had to spy on me? Peter either had his mind on the bet or else he wasn't quite sure of me. I didn't tell him she was to dine with me, as that was store business and no concern of his.

At that moment Smith opened the door and Carl Briggs came in. I knew him for an actor immediately. You can see hundreds of him on Broadway and Seventh Avenue in the neighborhood of the Palace Theatre. I suppose he was what is generally known as good-looking. He was masculine enough, heaven knows—the dark type—with a regularity of feature that probably took make-up very well. He was a big man. If there was a little less of everything he might have been one of those youths who pose for collars and underwear. He did have what is popularly known as sex appeal, I'm sure of that. His clothes, while not loud, were showy. His hair, which had a slight ripple, was pulled back away from his brow and was, I'm sure, held in place by some smelly sort of grease. He's one type who has never interested me. I'm confident with his clothes off he'd look a little like a fur rug. I've seen men like that on the beaches with hair all over them. By that I don't mean I dislike actors, hairy or otherwise. I've known many actors and actresses in my day and found them fascinating people, although they do talk a good bit about themselves—but, then, that is something that we have in common.

They were artists, serious about their work, who lived, breathed and adored the stage. When I think of the theater to-day and remember what it was I'm seized with longing and regret. The excitement and glamour have gone. There are no matinee idols any more. Of course, I do like Clark Gable; but, then, seeing him on a screen isn't the same as seeing James K. Hackett on the stage. There was a glamour about the flesh-and-blood person before you that the screen lacks. It's more true about the women than the men, too, I think. Perhaps the stage hasn't changed so much, after all, but it is the people who are different. No. It is the stage. I rarely ever see a play any more that I feel I can get my teeth into. Most of them are frothy fluff composed of some good smart wise-cracks. I think most playwrights to-day spend their time trying to outdo the other fellow for neat lines and let their plots go hang.

Carl Briggs, as he stood facing Peter, had that manner about him which announces itself with a capital I. I believe his type is commonly known in the profession as a "ham." Pork in any form has never been tasteful to me except sausage seasoned with sage. He made a good entrance, I'll say that for him, but it seemed quite as if he were playing a part.

"Where is she?" he asked dramatically.

For a moment I felt ashamed of my feelings. Ham or no ham, he undoubtedly loved his mother and was genuinely moved by the sudden news of her death. After all, he had seen her just a little while before, alive and well. While I was willing to give him the benefit of the doubt he didn't seem like a person who would be filled with filial affection or any other emotion which would not be of direct benefit to himself. If he hadn't killed her himself the news must have been a terrific shock.

"We've taken her away, Mr. Briggs," Peter said sympathetically. "Sit down."

"I can't, if you don't mind," Briggs answered. He paced up and down a minute and then asked, "Who did it?"

"We've no idea. There seems to be no reason for the crime, so far," Peter replied suggestively. "Perhaps you can furnish us with one."

"She's the last person in the world I'd expect to be murdered," Briggs answered, and I knew exactly what he meant. There are some people who seem fit victims for murder, nasty old men and oily preying young ones, flighty good-looking girls who get themselves into messes; but not a great mountain of flesh like Mrs. Briggs.

According to her son, Mrs. Briggs lived rather quietly with only one passion, her job at the store. She had worked for Doane's for nearly forty years, which led me to believe that he must be about thirty-five in spite of his efforts to look like a juvenile. His mother had a few intimate friends who dined or visited with her at her home because she did not go out very much. I could understand that. He didn't live with her, he said. He had a small apartment of his own. He gave acting as his occupation.

When asked about his visit to the store that morning he candidly admitted that he had come to borrow money. He offered as an excuse the scarcity of stage jobs. He had an interesting voice and I wondered why, if he was so hard up, he didn't work for the radio. They could do with good voices. I didn't know then the disdain a regular actor has for all radio work, unless of course he is a top-notcher and is commensurately paid for his valuable services.

He admitted that his mother had been cross and rather upset, but he didn't know why. He suggested that it was probably irritation due to the sale. Sales, he said, had always made her cross, and he probably knew that fact better than any one.

"You were here," Peter asked, "when your mother sent for Miss Sutton?"

"Yes."

"What did she say to Miss Sutton?"

"She gave her a bag of jewelry and told her to return it to stock. She was pretty mad and blamed Miss Sutton because most of the pieces came from her section."

"You know Miss Sutton quite well?" Peter suggested.

"I know most of the girls who work in the department," he admitted in a tone that implied he was irresistible to women.

"But don't you know Miss Sutton better than the others?" Peter insisted.

"I wouldn't say that." From under his heavy brows he seemed to be trying to determine just how much Peter knew.

"And Miss Oliver?" Peter suggested.

"Oh, her!" He dismissed Beth as easily as that.

"Why were you so long getting here?" Peter asked.

"I came as soon as I heard about it," he replied.

Peter let that pass and asked, "Who would want your mother dead, Mr. Briggs?"

I expected a denial. He didn't answer the question. He seemed suddenly divested of all his sham and pose. I would give my eye-teeth (mine happen to be false) to know what young Briggs was about to say. He looked at Peter, and I'm sure I saw the glint of real manhood in that glance. Just as he opened his mouth to speak it happened. I can't be sure that I heard the report of the gun because there was so much noise in the store, but it seems as if I did.

Carl Briggs' mouth opened. For a moment there was a look of incredible amazement on his face. He clutched at his chest with both hands and made a sound I'll never forget. Something that resembled an agonized "Ugh" escaped from his lips. Then he toppled forward.

I couldn't believe my own eyes. Peter was on his feet frantically calling for Smith. Davis popped up out of his chair and ran to the fallen man. I was a mass of quivers. To find a person already dead is bad enough, but to see a man alive and well one moment shot down before your eyes is a horrible experience. I often wondered why the men coming back from the war didn't talk about it. I think I know now.

Peter certainly was a man of action. At the door I heard him say to Smith. "I'm going up on that balcony. Briggs has been shot. Get a doctor. Hurry." I could hear his footsteps pounding down the corridor to the door at the side entrance.

For a second I saw the florid face of Mrs. Doyle peering in from behind the surprised Smith. I turned to see if I couldn't do something to help the wounded man. As I knelt beside Davis he turned to me and said in a softened voice. "I think he's dead."

# CHAPTER EIGHT

It was too much for me. As I have said, I've never been the fainting type, but I did feel all wrong inside as Davis pronounced the man dead. Perhaps the momentary dizziness came from leaning over so suddenly. At any rate my head was swimming and I did totter as I regained my feet. Davis put up a protecting hand to steady me. I'm rather sensitive about my ability to do things at my age and Davis' nice automatic gesture of help was a thrust at my vanity and I'm sure saved me from fainting.

"I'm all right," I managed to assure him; "it's just that I'm not accustomed to two murders in one day."

The band was playing rather frantically, I thought, trying to drown the tumult in the store. At that moment I wanted to get away. I didn't care about catching murderers or anything else. I wanted air, fresh air, not the store-laden type, which was heavy and dull and filled with noise and the blaring of that infernal band.

I went into the narrow corridor and hurried toward the side entrance. As I opened the door into the main part of the store I was facing the foot of the stairs which led to the balcony.

For those of you who are not familiar with the Doane store I will describe a little more, fully the first floor. You know about the small suite of offices at the right of the side entrance. On the left as you enter there is a staircase that leads to a balcony which parallels the side street and runs across the Avenue side of the store. As you reach the head of the stairs there is a small box-like office which has a door opening onto the balcony. Next to this office there is a string of elevators. Then come the telephone booths along the wall, and in front of them a number of chairs against the balcony rail. On the Avenue side in the corner nearest the telephone booths is the Personal Service department; then another lounging place for tired shoppers. This section is equipped with writing-desks and a post-office station. The balance of the balcony is devoted to a manicure parlor.

As I closed the corridor door I could hear some one crying hysterically behind me. For a moment I wondered if it was Mrs. Doyle wailing over the dead. At the head of the stairs as I looked up, I saw Beth Oliver standing beside Peter, who was rattling the knob of the little office trying to get inside. He stopped the working of the knob and put his shoulder to the door and began to push, bracing his feet on the heavy carpet. The door opened suddenly and Peter literally fell into the office.

It was too much for me. New excitement and a burning curiosity made me forget my momentary desire for air. I started up those stairs and pushed my way through the crowd at the top—you know how people herd when there is excitement of any kind. Beth Oliver was at the door. A group of women were crowding against her as I arrived.

I sailed through those startled women, making good use of my elbows to forge ahead. If I had not known the trick, memory of what I had seen at the store door that morning would have helped me. A surprise attack is always effective. As I reached Beth's side I gave her a slight shove, said, "Go in," and closed the door behind us.

There was a smell of powder in that room, but that wasn't what surprised me. Charlie Doane was standing there, looking, I thought, very blank for him.

"Well," Peter said, "what have you two to say for yourselves?"

"Why were you breaking in here ?" Charlie countered.

"You ought to know," Peter said accusingly.

"Don't let's talk in riddles," Charlie replied impatiently. "I just came down in the elevator when I heard you trying to break down the door. Why?"

We all turned to look, then, and sure enough in the

corner of the office there was the door of a small automatic elevator.

Peter scratched his head and made a quick survey of the room, which contained a flat desk, a telephone, two wooden armchairs and nothing else. The door to the automatic lift and the door onto the balcony were the only means of entrance or exit to the room.

Peter went to the elevator and pulled open its sliding door. He gave it a hasty but thorough search and then came back to us.

"I'll have to frisk you," he said to Charlie.

"All right, but why ?" Charlie asked, and with a wink at me he raised his arms over his head while Peter patted him from top to bottom, looking for a gun. Of course there wasn't any gun there.

When Peter had finished that operation Charlie said, "Now will you tell me what it's all about?"

"Just another try at murder," Peter said. "The woman's son this time."

"He's dead," I told them.

"What?" Charlie gasped.

"You sure?" Peter demanded.

"Oh, no!" Beth moaned.

I kicked out one of the chairs and sort of eased the girl into it. She was feeling pretty shaky at the moment.

"The shot came from this room," Peter stated definitely. I believed him because, as I say, I'm sure I smelled powder when I stepped through the door.

"But how could it?" Charlie protested.

"That's what I'll have to find out," Peter reminded him grimly.

There was a rap on the door.

"Who is it?" Peter snapped.

"McLeod," the voice answered. "Anything wrong here? Step back, please." We could hear him admonishing the crowd.

Peter let him in. "Go down and send my man Smith up here at once. Get the people away from this door and see that the body down there is properly guarded," he ordered all in one breath.

As Sandy left, Charlie said, "Had you noticed this?" He walked across the room and opened a small circular window in the side partition. Opened, it looked like a porthole, a small one.

"Why did you touch it?" Peter complained.

"I'm wearing gloves," Charlie answered.

"So you are."

I didn't like the tone of Peter's voice. Was he suspecting Charlie of this murder just as he was inclined to suspect Beth of the other one? We all of us defend ourselves unnecessarily at times. Charlie didn't have to explain then, but he did.

"I was on my way to lunch when I let you in," he said.

I hadn't realized before that he was wearing a hat.

Smith came at that moment.

Peter's orders were fast and furious. "I want the bottom of this elevator shaft searched for a gun. Send a man here at once; I'll tell him what to do. Get going.

"Now," Peter turned to Charlie, "tell me your story."

"I left my office on the sixth floor, which is right next to the entrance to this elevator. I pushed the button and the 'In Use' sign flashed on. I could hear the purr of the cables. The light went off for a second. I pushed the button again and the 'In Use' sign flashed once more. I waited not more than a second or two and heard the car coming up to my floor. When the car arrived I came down at once and heard you trying to get in here. That's all there is to tell."

"Isn't it pretty late to be going to lunch ?" Peter asked, and I could have slapped him for his intimation.

"Yes, rather," Charlie answered. "I was going over some figures," he looked at me, "and lost all track of time."

I suddenly remembered that I had had no lunch, if you can call what I eat luncheon. I have a few lettuce leaves and either a pear or a tomato. Most people eat too

much, anyhow. One good meal a day is all I need and I
have that at night.

"What's the idea of this thing, anyhow?" Peter asked,
pointing to the lift, and although I hadn't forgiven him for
suspecting Charlie I did feel sorry for him, just the same.
One murder in a day ought to be enough for even a
policeman, but when you get two of them and one done
practically under your very nose, it is a bit thick. I knew
Peter would be in for a grilling from his superiors, though
for the life of me, I don't see what he could have done
about it.

"The elevator, you mean?" Charlie said.

"Yes," Peter answered.

"It was an idea of my father's," Charlie explained. "He
loved this store and everything about it. When this new
building was planned, Father had this private shaft put
in for his use and the use of store executives. He rode
down in it every morning and stood on the balcony at the
head of the stairs and said a few words to the employees."

"Every morning?" Peter asked.

Charlie nodded a little shamefacedly, I thought. "Yes.
Ten minutes before opening time the employees gathered
on the main floor and sang for about three minutes, then
Father spoke to them for another three, which gave them
four minutes to get back to their posts before the doors
were opened."

"Sounds like a Rotary Club luncheon I once went to,"
Peter said.

"The same idea," Charlie agreed.

For the life of me I didn't know whether Peter was
serious about the Rotary Club idea or not. I've always
meant to ask him; but it slipped my mind at the time. It's
no mystery to me that all men are boys in various stages
of development and I suppose if they want to get together,
sing songs and slap each other on the back as they yell
"Hello, Bill!" or "Hi, Jerry!" it's perfectly all right. It
certainly is no worse than the weird outfits they wear
when a group of Shriners, I believe they are called, get

together. Personally, I never had much use for Robert
Doane or his ideas. He was one of those serious young
men born to get ahead in the world and have no fun while
doing it. After all his years of struggle he left a huge
store, a no-account daughter and a son who didn't care for
the business. But, then, I don't suppose he could help
being stuffy.

"How about that porthole?" Peter demanded

"That was another of Father's ideas," Charlie
explained. "He would stand in front of that little window
by the hour watching the store and the people."

"Sort of a spy-glass?" Peter suggested.

"I don't think that was his intention. I can't say."
Charlie's voice mumbled away to nothing.

An officer tapped on the door. He was one of Peter's
men sent up by Sandy. Peter admitted him.

"See that?" Peter pointed to the elevator. "Get Bayard.
Have him go over it for fingerprints. When he has
finished I want you to go up in it and stop at every floor
between here and the top. Take Bayard with you. See if
you can find any prints on each of the doors. Stop and ask
questions. I want to know who used the pesky thing,
coming and going, in the last fifteen minutes."

Peter went back to the porthole. It was open just as
Charlie had left it. He put his face to it and jerked back.
He repeated the operation several times until I thought
he had been suddenly bereft of his senses.

"Did you know about this?" he turned and asked
Charlie.

"I just told you that you could see most of the main
floor."

"I don't mean that. You can hear voices," he explained.

Then I was sure he was mad.

"Voices?" I asked, and moved away from Beth to join
Charlie, who had stepped closer to Peter.

As you approached that little window and stood with
your face about three inches from the opening you
certainly could hear voices. It was a most unaccountable

experience. It sounded exactly as if people were talking just outside the partition. The three of us crowded together and listened.

"Are you feeling better now?" a voice asked.

The voice topped a low hiccoughing sobbing. We all looked down at the same time. From our vantage-point we could see into the three small offices. Carl Briggs was stretched on the floor just as I had left him. Eva Sutton sat in a chair looking down at the body while a doctor worked over him. The store nurse was there, standing beside Eva Sutton, with that impersonality which only nurses can assume in the face of anything. Things had happened so fast. I was so completely bowled over by Carl Briggs' murder that I hadn't stopped to think about the why of it. That little port-hole explained a lot of things. I was so certain that Briggs, as he stood facing Peter, was about to tell us something of importance that I was doubly amazed when he toppled over clutching at his chest. The idea struck Peter and myself at the same time. Whoever it was who had been standing at that little porthole, thanks no doubt to a crazy freak of store construction and acoustics, had heard everything that had been said in the office. Carl Briggs had been shot to keep him from talking.

I'm sure the listening window was not planned by old Robert Doane. I don't believe he would have stooped to such a trick, but I'll bet when he discovered it worked he stood there doing as much listening as looking. Men talk about women, but they themselves are born snoops and gossips.

The officer and Bayard rapped on the door and were admitted.

"Get anything you can find on here first," Peter instructed, indicating the little window as we moved away from it.

Beth stood up. "May I go?" she asked.

"What were you doing on the balcony?" Peter asked without answering her question.

"I came to see Mr. Doane," she answered.

You could have knocked me down with a feather. I always knew Charlie went after anything he wanted, but somehow the idea of his meeting the girl in the store like that bothered me.

"Just a moment," Charlie spoke up. "Did I understand you to say you came here to see me?"

"Isn't that what you said?" she asked.

There was something there which I didn't understand; neither did they, by the look of them.

"Let's begin all over again," Peter suggested to Beth; "Mr. Doane seems a little confused."

"About ten minutes ago I was called to the telephone in the department," she explained. "A man's voice, he said it was you," she looked at Charlie, "asked me to meet him in the private office on the balcony at the head of the stairs. That's all."

"But I didn't telephone you!" Charlie denied, and I'll admit I felt better about him.

"Wait a minute," Peter broke in. "I think I see it I wouldn't leave the store if I were you, Mr. Doane; I may want you. Can't you eat in here somewhere?"

"Certainly," Charlie replied. "How about you, Ethel; would you like a cup of tea?"

"I'd like a highball right now," I replied.

"In my office, after five-thirty," he grinned at me. "We don't serve liquor in the store, although we do sell it in bottles."

"Another of Father's ideas, I suppose," I said. Then I wanted to make up to him for my suspicions of the previous moment. "Take Miss Oliver with you. She could do with a cup of tea, I'm sure. You haven't had any lunch, have you?" I asked her, rather fiercely, I'm afraid.

"I mustn't take the time," she offered by way of an excuse. I was wrong about the girl. If she was planning to capture Charlie, she would have jumped at the chance.

Charlie smiled in that nice way he has. When he exerts his charm, he is the nicest person I know. "For the second time to-day, Miss Oliver," he began, "I'll have to give you an order. Unless you come with me and have some luncheon, so you can do your work properly," he said with mock seriousness, "I'm afraid I'll have to dismiss you from the store. You are no good to us unless you can do your work. The store comes first, you know." He turned to Peter, "We'll be in the main floor tea-room. Then I'm sending Miss Oliver home."

"Miss Oliver can't go home," Peter said grimly.

"But—" Charlie began a protest.

"Sorry." Peter included both of them. "I know Miss Oliver has had two severe shocks, but this is murder and it makes a difference. I don't care what she does with her time, but I don't want her to leave the store until I say so—you either, for that matter."

"I'll be all right," Beth said to Charlie, and then turned to Peter. "I'll be in the department when you want me."

She was brave. The average person in her position would have wanted to leave the store immediately after Mrs. Briggs' death because of the emotional upset. If you have lived with a person, their sudden death does something to you; you don't have to love them to be affected. She had been carrying on, a quality which I have always admired in man or woman.

I gave the girl a gentle shove toward Charlie. "Thank you," she said.

As Charlie held the door open for her to pass through I whispered to him, "Be careful." Why, I know not unless it was a premonition.

He scowled a warning to be quiet and stepped onto the balcony behind Beth. A little later Peter came over and held the door open for me. From the balcony I could see Beth and Charlie headed for the tea-room in the annex. Peter was in a hurry to get back to Briggs. I toddled along behind him fairly tripping down the steps. My thoughts kept pace with my feet. Two murders in one morning; open daring murders, committed within the

sight and sound of hundreds of people. Why? Why on a
Sales Day of all days? Why this rush to kill people? What
made Mrs. Briggs' death so imperative, and what would
Carl Briggs have told us if he had been permitted to live
another minute or two? Carl Briggs had not killed his
mother.

What was the reason behind these two deaths? I felt
something more than curiosity as I trailed Peter into the
little corridor. Being a woman I would call it a
premonition. I know that's old-fashioned, but you can't
convince a woman that it isn't true, just the same. I
couldn't possibly have known of the twisted course events
were to take before five o'clock, but I felt afraid
nevertheless. Why was the Sutton girl in there looking so
distractedly at the body of Carl Briggs?

Peter called Smith and told him to check with the
store telephone department on the call Beth said she had
received from Charlie. Peter said, "Locate that call and
the person who made it if you can."

Smith went to a telephone at once.

Herbert, John Grover, Banter and Kramer were
cluttering the narrow corridor just outside of Mrs. Curtis'
office where the body lay.

"What does this mean?" Herbert asked.

"A cover up job to hide the first murder," Peter
snapped.

"Is he dead?" Banter asked.

"Want any help?" Kramer offered his services.

"There's nothing any of you can do. If I want you I'll
let you know. You're really in the way. I wish you'd clear
out and give my men a free hand."

They started to go, trailing off somewhat like whipped
dogs, when Peter stopped Kramer. "I wish you'd locate
William Evans for me."

"We'll do it at once," Grover answered for Kramer, "if
we can."

# CHAPTER NINE

When I followed Peter into the office Eva Sutton was still there sitting in the chair looking down at Briggs. She clasped and unclasped her hands hopelessly. She was quiet except for a recurrent heart-racking sob which seemed to shake her entire poor little body. I felt sorry for her. I didn't know what the Briggs man meant to her or why she was sobbing like that. The poor thing seemed numbed and dazed, and no wonder, two murders in sudden succession are enough to upset any one.

"What are you doing here?" Peter asked.

"I came in when I heard the shot," she replied listlessly. Her mind seemed to be engrossed in some problem of her own.

"Then you expected something to happen?" Peter asked pointedly.

"I just heard the shot." She was vaguely inattentive to Peter.

"And you ran in to see what had happened to Briggs? Is that it?" Peter tried to get through her stoniness.

She nodded.

"But why?"

"I don't know. I had a feeling." She stopped and looked up at Peter. "I can't talk to you now, I'm— I can't think straight." She was pathetic.

"I'll talk to you later." Peter turned to the nurse. "Take her away," he instructed.

At Peter's suggestion the nurse took hold of the girl's arm to lead her away. For a fleeting moment I wondered how the department was working with two of the women, no, three of them, not there to check every sale which was being made. I was beginning to be store-minded, and no wonder, I had heard so much store all day long.

The nurse tugged at Eva's arm, which roused the girl

from her befuddled mental state. For a moment her eyes were blank. Then fear welled back into them. She yanked her arm out of the nurse's grasp and said to Peter, "Let me stay here with you. Don't send me away, please!"

"Sorry," he said kindly, "but you must go."

"I don't want to go!" she wailed.

"The nurse will take good care of you." He nodded to the nurse again.

"I won't go! You can't make me! I'm not going to be killed too!"

"There, there." The nurse tried to quiet her.

"Who would want to kill you?" Peter asked.

"They—" She moaned. "Why did they kill him?" She pointed at the prone body.

I followed the direction of her fingers. My glance at the corpse gave me the queerest feeling. Carl Briggs looked different stretched there in death. There was something vaguely familiar about him, something which I had not noticed before. Death had robbed him of his personality. The shell of what had once been a man reminded me of some one I had known and yet I couldn't remember.

"Who are 'they'?" Peter asked.

"The murderers," she replied in a lowered voice.

"Are there more than one?" Peter asked quickly. It was a neat question, gauged to trap the girl.

"How do I know?" she asked without guile.

Peter braced himself squarely in front of her and demanded harshly, "Just what do you know?" She refused to look at him. "Out with it!" Peter insisted.

"You're too interested in all this to be entirely innocent."

"If I knew I'd tell you," she said after a moment.

"Why are you afraid?" he demanded; his patience showed signs of fraying.

"Because—" She stopped stubbornly.

"Are you going to tell me?" His voice was keen with annoyance.

"No." It was a flat defiant refusal.

"Do you want to be arrested?" he threatened.

If he hoped to frighten her he failed, because she replied, "I don't care. I'd be safe." The poor thing was completely overwrought. She bit her lips and pulled at her handkerchief when she wasn't daubing her eyes to keep the tears back. "Please don't send me back there!" she pleaded, "I don't want to die."

Peter was stumped. "I'll take care of you," he promised with assurance, "if you'll tell me what you fear. I can't protect you from a danger I don't understand."

"You didn't protect him." She pointed to Briggs and there was no answer to that, but Peter replied immediately,

"I didn't know Briggs was in danger. Did you?" He shot the question at her.

"I—er," she stammered and stopped. I could almost hear that girl think as she looked at Peter with a speculative glint in her eyes. She had managed to get herself caught in a net and she was trying to think of a way out.

"Well?" Peter's insistence was relentless.

"There were reasons for his death," she said slowly, still marshaling her thoughts.

"That's evident," Peter growled impatiently, "but what?"

"The people who knew about Carl. Her," she pointed her finger at me, "Mr. Doane, Oliver and Mr. Hastings. They all knew."

"Knew what?" I snapped at the girl. What on earth was she driving at? She was very cleverly shifting attention from herself.

"Are you accusing Miss Thomas of murder?" Peter asked.

"Why is she here?" the girl retorted, getting to her feet.

"Sit down," Peter commanded. "Now tell me what you mean?"

It was a sordid story. The sort of thing you read about more often than you meet as an experience. Anna Briggs had been a beautiful young woman working in Doane's store. Robert, whose wife became an invalid after Gladys was born, went a-maying soon after that. Mrs. Briggs, who had just been widowed, became the object of his affections. Carl was the result of that second sowing. I did some rapid calculations, as a person will on hearing such a story, and realized that Gladys was thirty-five. I had been wrong about the Briggs boy. He was probably only thirty-one or thirty-two. I was allowing perhaps longer than necessary for decency. I believed the girl's story. As Carl Briggs lay there on the floor, he was an overripe image of what Robert Doane had been as a younger man. That's what I had tried to determine as I vaguely recognized something just a few minutes before.

Robert Doane. I didn't think he had it in him. You never can tell about a man and least of all about the quiet, serious type. I'm not blaming him. I knew his wife too well. She enjoyed her ill health to a fairly ripe old age. She was the sighing, weepy type of invalid. I called on her a few times, but lost my patience and stopped going.

Doane and Mrs. Briggs were warm friends up to the time of his death. Eva Sutton said that Doane had given Mrs. Briggs money for her and Carl. That, if true, may explain why he didn't have more cash when he died.

When Peter asked her how she knew all that, her answer was reasonable enough.

She said that people in the store knew about it. She asked, and her question was logical enough, "Why do you suppose they kept such a big fat woman on in the store?"

I hadn't thought of that angle. Eva Sutton said the store executives knew about Mrs. Briggs and Robert. After Robert's death they didn't dare dismiss her. She also went on to say that Carl Briggs had discovered the truth and was going to claim his rights. Carl wanted some of the money which had been left to his mother. The mother was either frugal or perhaps she didn't trust Carl;

at any rate, she kept a tight rein on the purse-strings. Carl was building up a case against the store, determined to bring suit in the courts unless his mother gave him the money he felt was rightly his.

They had been arguing about it that morning when she had been sent for. Eva admitted listening.

"What did you hear?" Peter asked.

"Mrs. Briggs told him she had to be careful of the money because now that Charlie Doane was back she'd probably lose her job."

I groaned inwardly, remembering what Banter or Grover had said earlier in the morning. Charlie had wanted to discharge the poor soul. Peter evidently remembered it too.

"So she knew she was going to be fired, eh?" he asked.

"She seemed to be sure of it," the girl replied. "It's very funny," she went on and not without reason, "that they should both be killed just at the moment Carl had his plans ready for a suit. They are all in the plot." There was meanness in her eyes as she looked at me accusingly. "Why don't you ask the Oliver girl what she was doing in that little office just before Carl was shot?"

"How do you know she was in there?" he asked.

"Because I looked up and saw her coming out of the door just before I heard the commotion in here."

"It's utter nonsense," I assured Peter.

"I wouldn't be too sure of that," he answered seriously.

"If it's such nonsense," she turned to me, "why were they both killed?"

"That is what Mr. Conklin is trying to find out," I answered. "Charlie Doane didn't kill either one of them, and you know it." I turned to Peter to see if he believed me.

"He seems to be able to get himself into suspicious places, just the same," Peter replied.

"I don't believe Charlie Doane even knows this story," I went on with my defense.

"Huh!" The girl's doubt was scathing.

"How do you know so much about this?" I turned on the girl, controlling my desire to throttle her. "Who gave you your information? What was Briggs to you?"

"I've known Carl Briggs a long time," she replied promptly, defiance of me in her eyes. "We were just friends."

"So he confided his private affairs to you?" I didn't try to keep the sneer out of my voice.

"He had to talk to some one. Could I help it if he told me things?" she asked defensively.

"Why do you keep talking in riddles?" Peter demanded. "If you know anything, spill it."

"I didn't talk before because I didn't want to be fired," she sobbed; "but I don't care now. I'd rather lose my job than be badgered about. Mr. Doane didn't want the scandal to come out because he's doing the same thing his father done."

It wasn't her bad grammar that made me gasp; it was the thing she implied.

"What are you talking about?" Peter really growled.

"Oliver and Mr. Doane. The whole store is talking about it. Mr. Doane's only been back in the store a little while and yet he's been trying to take his half-brother's wife away from him. Like father, like son, they've been saying. It's bad enough to be cheated out of your inheritance, but when you're going to lose your wife as well, you can't blame a man for being mad."

"You're sure of this?" Peter asked.

Eva Sutton was calmly calculating as she went on talking. She turned her defiant eyes toward me once in a while.

"That's why I want to be protected," she said. "They know I know too much. They got rid of the old lady first, and then Carl, which avoided a scandal and made Oliver free to marry Mr. Doane."

"This is a serious charge you're making," Peter warned.

"I know it," she replied, "and I don't care, if you will

protect me."

"I'll send a man with you to the department. Keep mum. We'll take care of you. I'll need you later."

The girl was taken away.

I knew the things she had said were utter rot. I didn't believe Charlie knew the story of his father's affair, but I did know that Charlie believed himself in love with Beth. Beth. Why under the sun hadn't she told Peter the story she was keeping for me? Drat her, anyhow! Her silence was going to make things worse for both of them. She had added grist to Peter's mill by keeping silent.

"Now we're getting places." There was triumph in Peter's voice.

I was thinking about Herbert Hastings. The store had been his life ever since he had entered into it. I felt at the time of the wedding that he was marrying the store and not Gladys. The name of Doane had grown to mean a great deal to Herbert. Having no background of his own, he had lived in the reflected light of the Doane name. He'd do anything to protect the store and keep the name of Doane clean, I was sure of that, but somehow I didn't think he'd go as far as murder.

"It's odd," Peter said, "the way the Oliver girl keeps popping into the picture."

"You're a nitwit, Peter Conklin," I accused, completely out of patience with him.

"I believe you're right," he said. "Suppose we think out-loud for a moment, you and I."

"Sort of clear the fog?" I asked.

"It might. You know these people better than I do and obviously you want to protect them. We can begin at the beginning."

"It's a waste of time," I said tartly. "The criminal has had too much time already."

"You sound like the Police Commissioner," he smiled wryly.

"How about this Willie person?" I asked. "Did you get anything from him?"

"By George!" he exclaimed. "I'd forgotten all about him. We have been sort of busy," he reminded me needlessly. "Smith," he called over the partition, "get that man from the receiving-room!"

"He hasn't come back," Smith answered from the door. "They don't know what has happened to him. He's never done it before, they say."

"Send some one to his home. I want that man. Also ask Mr. Hastings to come down here."

"I have the other reports for you," Smith said.

"Send a man to find Willie and come back," Peter commanded.

Smith had papers in his hand when he came back. Peter read the notes to me. The telephone call to Beth Oliver came from the private office on the balcony. Peter was almost gleeful in his satisfaction.

"Wrong," I insisted. "If the things the Sutton girl says were true—and they're not," I added, "Charlie Doane wouldn't call her to that office and implicate her in the man's murder."

"You have a way of smacking a nail on the head," he admitted. "Who called her?"

"Doesn't your report say?"

"The operator doesn't know, only remembers making the connection."

"Too bad." I'm afraid I sneered.

"Yes, isn't it?" he replied. "How do you like this?" He read from Smith's report. " 'Beth Oliver registered, at the address given, last night under her own name. There was a package for her at the desk, delivered this morning. The package contained jewelry.'"

"Obviously a plant," I said immediately.

"By whom?" he asked.

"That's your business," I retorted.

"And how!" he replied with satisfaction.

Peter went on with the report. Eva Sutton had an expensive apartment in the Fifties. Peter arched his eyes at me. Nothing incriminating was found there.

"It doesn't coincide with her fear of losing her job," I said pointedly.

"It will bear some investigation," he replied. "We are beginning to get into things now." There was relish in his voice.

"That girl has something she is hiding," I said definitely.

"Miss Oliver?" he asked, knowing very well what I meant.

"No," I snapped. "Eva Sutton. She told us about Mrs. Briggs to divert attention from herself."

"Perhaps." He went on reading the report.

There were no fingerprints in Mrs. Briggs' office that were distinguishable except Beth Oliver's and those of the dead woman. I was beginning to doubt the efficacy of fingerprints in solving crimes.

When Peter had finished with the last of the reports he sent Smith away and grunted. "You see," he said, "how exciting a man-hunt can be when you really begin to get going. We had two crimes and no tangible evidence, but now we are going places. I've got a case at last and a motive."

"You've got wild ideas. You're so wrong." Trying to convince him was like shoveling sand against the tide.

"The Oliver girl killed the old dame and then your friend killed the son to cover her," he said. He had convinced himself that he was right at last.

"What are you going to do?" I asked. He was so smug and I felt so helpless.

"Work with the material I have at hand," he answered. "We have a fairly good motive now and a little circumstantial evidence will help us a lot. Your friend Mr. Doane didn't want any scandal. He wanted to get Mrs. Briggs out of the store. We know he planned her dismissal. He had a talk with her either last night or this morning. They couldn't reach any reasonable understanding. Doane was worried. He told Miss Oliver all about it. She wanted to help him." He considered for a moment. "Yes, it all fits together. Miss Oliver came in here this morning, killed the woman and then tried to cover herself by implicating young Briggs. She was clever. She fooled you and she fooled me for a time."

"How did she kill Mrs. Briggs?" I interrupted to ask.

"We'll get to that later. She carried the implement away with her," Peter replied patly. A man can be so annoying when he thinks he's right. He went on, "Charles Doane knew about the little whispering window. He was worried. He knew we were going to question Carl Briggs. Doane watched and listened at that window. When he was sure that Briggs was going to tip the story, Doane fired the shot."

"What did he do with the gun?" I asked. "He didn't have it on him; you searched him yourself. And what about that telephone call for Miss Oliver? He wouldn't have done that."

"Sure he would. That was part of his scheme to give him an alibi."

"But he denies calling her," I protested futilely. "He's a gentleman; don't forget that."

"And a fast worker," he assured me. "Men like Doane don't usually take girls like Miss Oliver to lunch in their own store. They save that for little apartments somewhere on Riverside Drive."

"Isn't Park Avenue the street of kept women now?" I asked with as much naiveté as I could manage.

"Depends on the girl and the man's income," Peter came right back.

"I suggested he take her to lunch," I reminded him.

"And Doane jumped at the chance, too. He wanted a little time to think. He's in a spot, with all this scandal brewing. The papers will love it. Maybe he did both murders, the first to hush the scandal and the second to get the girl."

"You don't know Charlie Doane," I insisted. "If he knows about this chapter in his father's life he'd do all that he could to make amends."

For the second or third time that day he said, "That's what you think." An expression which has always nettled me. Some words and phrases jar me. "So what," a recent contribution to our slang, is another of them.

There are some colloquialisms which I use and like because they are so expressive. Then, too, one must resort to slang occasionally if one hopes to be understood. Pure speech these days is about as rare as virgins in front of the library lions at Fifth Avenue and Forty-second Street.

I didn't answer Peter. He stood up, stretched and said he'd have to see the reporters or they would begin to give him the old raspberry. I asked him about that and he said it was the same as the Bronx cheer. I still didn't know. He demonstrated for me. I must say the idea is expressive if not altogether delicate.

I visualized the headlines in the afternoon papers telling all about the death of the ex-mistress of Robert Doane—Son Suspected—and all that horrible stuff.

"You're not going to put in all the things you've just told me, are you?" I asked fearfully.

"I'll tell them there have been two murders and we report progress and hope to have the guilty party late this afternoon. That'll give the boys an extra, which is just what they want."

She'd gone completely out of my mind up to that moment. "Where's Mrs. Doyle?" I asked.

"Who?"

"The woman I told you about. We've kept her waiting a long time."

When asked, Smith said he hadn't seen the woman since the second murder. I was annoyed and showed it.

"See how we lose witnesses in this case," Peter taunted. "Willie and now your Mrs. Doyle."

I was stubborn about that woman. She had been nearer to the scene of the first crime than any one we had questioned up to then. Bother her, anyhow! Why couldn't she have waited? I went to the telephone and asked for Sandy and told him to find Mrs. Doyle again.

"You'll never find her," Peter comforted me when I hung up.

"I'll find her if I have to turn New York inside out," I vowed.

"Just tell me how you'd do that. I'd like to know—I have a couple of problems on my hands, too."

I was doing some fast thinking. What paper would Mrs. Doyle be likely to read? One of the scandal sheets, obviously. I couldn't imagine her reading the *Times, Sun* or the *Tribune*. Well, that was that. How to get at her through the paper?

"What's the plan?" he urged.

"Peter," I began, "a woman like that probably reads the scandal sheets or the tabloids. Couldn't you get the reporters to run a story about her, asking her to come back to the store?"

"I might, but why do you think she's so important?"

"Peter," I begged, "don't give what you have just heard to the press until you are sure, please. It can do no harm for you to wait a little while. You are wrong. If I could only prove it to you! Do you want to ruin your career by making a fatal mistake?"

"Stop," he said with a twinkle in his eyes; "you're breaking my heart."

I knew he was spoofing me, but I was far too serious to be able to respond to his jocular mood. I told him about my meeting with Mrs. Doyle early in the morning. I told him about sending her to that little door.

"Just believe that Beth Oliver is telling the truth," I reasoned. "We know she came down in the rear elevator a little after nine. Eva Sutton saw her."

"So what?"

I ignored that and went on, because it dawned on me then that he was pulling my leg, but I had to be sure he'd keep Eva Sutton's story out of the papers.

"Your man Willie, Eva Sutton and Carl Briggs were in the receiving-room and saw Beth. We are reasonably sure that the murder of Mrs. Briggs took place very close to nine o'clock. If the murderer had gone through the receiving-room on his way out, four people would have seen him. He didn't; he must have gone by the door which Mrs. Doyle used. You can't find Willie. He must have seen the murderer go into Mrs. Briggs' office. We've checked all the people who used the door into the book department, haven't we?"

He nodded.

"It was just after nine when Mrs. Doyle went through that door. If any one in the world saw the murderer she's the person. Isn't a story from her worth trying before you do something which I know you'll regret later?"

"Why didn't you tell me this before ?" He was boiling mad.

"Because at first I didn't think about her and then when I did I wanted to surprise you."

"You've done that, all right," he threw at me over his shoulder as he dashed toward the door and collided with Herbert Hastings.

# CHAPTER TEN

Herbert's dignity had taken a jolting along with the physical impact of Peter's body. I was glad of it. I don't know why I feel the way I do about Herbert Hastings. Just contrariness, I guess. He's always been nice enough. Too nice, I suppose that's the answer. He has always acted as if I were an intractable child. I suppose I have been hard to handle, in one sense of the word, but I certainly don't need the guidance of people like Herbert. If he had only accepted me for what I am I'd probably have felt differently toward him. He needed friendship and understanding, heaven knows, being married to Gladys, but he never had that free and easy air with me that Charlie has always had even from a youngster. Herbert, I think, is and has been afraid of me and because of that I'm just mean enough to keep on saying boo to him. People do invite much of the treatment they receive from their fellows.

Peter backed away from him and said, "I'd forgotten I sent for you. Sit down."

"I came at once," Herbert said. "Wasn't it important?" He sat down facing Peter.

"How long have you been connected with Doane's?" Peter asked.

"About fifteen years," Herbert replied.

"You've known Mrs. Briggs for a long time, then?"

"She's been a figure in the store, one of the fixtures— what is known as an old-timer." Herbert essayed a weak smile.

"You knew about Mrs. Briggs and Mr. Doane?" Peter went directly to the point.

Herbert looked down as he said, "Yes."

"A number of store people, I believe, knew about it,"

Peter went on.

Again Herbert replied with a demure, "Yes."

"Do you know any reason why Mrs. Briggs should have been murdered?" Peter demanded.

"None," Herbert replied immediately.

"She was an old woman, fat, unable to get about. Why did you keep her on?" Peter shot the question at him.

"She did her work well," Herbert answered.

"Don't evade the question, Mr. Hastings." There was a warning note in Peter's voice.

"It was understood that she was to have a position in the store as long as she wanted it," Herbert answered.

"Understood by whom?"

"Mr. Doane expressed that wish just shortly before he died," Herbert said, and I must admit he seemed reluctant to say it.

"Then you've been carrying out the wishes of a dead man?"

"Yes."

"How did you feel about Mr. Charles Doane's suggestion that Mrs. Briggs be let go?"

"I didn't know what to say."

I was pleased to hear that remark. It was practically an admission that Charlie didn't know about his father's connection with Mrs. Briggs.

"Did you try to dissuade him?"

"No."

"Why not?"

"Because—" Herbert began, and stopped.

"I know all about it, Herbert," I said. "I won't be shocked by anything you may have to say."

"It was rather a delicate subject," Herbert began. "I didn't want to discuss it with him, and yet at the same time the Briggs situation was getting to be a bit difficult."

"In what way?"

"Most of our shortages were from her department, for one thing, and her son was getting difficult," Herbert explained.

"What about the son?" Peter asked.

"He threatened to bring suit against the store."

"On what grounds?"

"He claimed to be the son of Robert Doane. Of course that was ridiculous, but in the light of what everyone knew, it would have been a terrible scandal. He wanted to blackmail us, I'm sure."

"Did you ever give him any money?"

"Once."

Peter pounced on him for that. "Why, if you were so sure there was no foundation for his claim, were you willing to give him money?"

"I didn't want any scandal. The whole sordid mess would have been accepted by the press as the truth. The name of Doane and the reputation of the store would have been sullied."

"Don't you know giving money to a blackmailer is a serious mistake?" Peter asked contemptuously.

"I know it now."

"You knew it then," I cut in. "Carl Briggs is the image of Robert Doane as a young man."

He turned to me and said, "I didn't know Mr. Doane when he was a young man."

That was true, he didn't. I had forgotten the difference in our ages.

"When was the last time you saw young Briggs?"

"Yesterday," Herbert answered.

"Was he after money again?"

"Yes. He wanted to see Charlie Doane, but I circumvented that."

"Then Mr. Doane knows about this old scandal?"

"I don't know."

"Why did you keep Briggs from seeing him?"

"Mr. Doane has a hot temper; all the Doanes have. I feared the consequences of a meeting between them."

What Herbert said was true enough, but I didn't like the implication in the way he said it.

"Did you ever discuss her son with Mrs. Briggs?"

"Yesterday after he left my office."

"What did she have to say about him?"

"She assured me she would keep him quiet."

"Has Charles Doane ever done or said anything which would lead you to believe that he knew about the Briggs scandal?"

"Never. That's why I was worried when he wanted to pension Mrs. Briggs. I was afraid it might come out."

"I'm looking for a motive, Mr. Hastings. Up to the time young Briggs was shot there were one or two reasons why the woman was killed. With Briggs murdered we have a slightly different aspect to the case. You might have killed them both to avoid a scandal."

"I wouldn't do that." Herbert accepted the accusation and answered it fairly enough.

"What is going on in the store, Mr. Hastings?" Peter asked.

"What do you mean?"

"Who or what group of people in the store would want the Briggs woman out of the way?"

"I don't know."

"If the death of Mrs. Briggs is connected with the store in any way, how does young Briggs enter into it?"

"I can't answer that, either." Herbert seemed puzzled.

"Did you ever have any reason to suspect Mrs. Briggs herself in connection with the shortages you mention?"

"Oh, no! She was absolutely honest."

"If there was anything crooked going on in the store, would you know about it?" Peter asked.

"It would be brought to my notice eventually," he replied.

"Have you any explanations about the shortages?"

"None whatever."

"Did you discuss her shortages with Mrs. Briggs?"

"Often."

"Did she ever advance any theory?"

"No, but she assured me yesterday that she would get to the bottom of them or die trying."

"I wonder if she did?" Peter mused.

"Did what?" I asked.

"Died trying," he replied.

"You don't die trying in a case like that," I answered. "She died because her trying was successful."

"You'll keep this family scandal out of the papers, won't you?" Herbert asked uneasily as he prepared to go-

"It won't be mentioned unless it has something to do with the murder," Peter assured him.

When Herbert was out of hearing, I said gleefully to Peter, "I told you Charlie Doane knew nothing about this scandal!"

"Maybe you're right. I'm going out now to have a talk with the reporters. I'll try to locate your old lady for you. See you later."

"You won't tell them about Charlie and the scandal?" I begged.

"Not until I have a talk with Charlie Doane and the Oliver girl. I'll see them as soon as I get through with the reporters."

"Don't let what Herbert said about the Doane tempers influence you," I urged. I regretted it the moment I had said it.

# CHAPTER ELEVEN

I wanted to see Charlie. If he had to know about his father's derelictions I wanted to be the one to tell him. I had some other things to tell him as well. I didn't want him to be knocked out by the news of Beth's marriage to Carl Briggs and all the things it implied.

Beth was in the jewelry department looking much better. I stopped at her counter, wondering what she was thinking and feeling. Across the aisle I saw Eva Sutton scowling at us. I leaned forward and said, "Peter Conklin now thinks Charlie Doane killed young Briggs so he could marry you."

"He couldn't think that," she replied, amazed. "It's beyond reason."

"Do you know that the whole store has been talking about you and Mr. Charles Doane?" I demanded.

"I hardly know Mr. Doane. Why should they?"

"Don't ask me riddles. I'm telling you facts. Eva Sutton has been telling things to Peter Conklin." I remembered her accusation and asked, "Were you in that room at the head of the stairs?"

Beth repeated the story she had told Peter. I believed her. She was probably turning away from the door with her hand on the knob when the Sutton girl, looking up from a distance, saw her and decided that she was closing the door behind her.

Beth looked at me and asked, "You don't believe these stories, do you?"

"Certainly not. Do you think I'm a fool ? What I think isn't important. It's what Peter thinks and the papers say, that we must worry about now—scandal," I finished.

"I'm sorry; believe me, I am."

The poor thing looked it. I reached out and gave her a

reassuring pat on the arm. "I'll see you through this, don't you worry. Now call Charlie Doane for me and tell him to meet me on the main floor in front of the central elevators right away. I've got to talk to him."

She reached for the telephone. "Sit tight," I advised. "It's bound to be all right."

I waited until she finished telephoning. People who insist upon talking to you while you are trying to converse over the telephone ought to be shot at the first offense.

"He'll be down," she said.

"The Sutton girl hates you. Why?" I asked with absolutely no consideration of her feelings.

"I don't believe it's hate," she said thoughtfully. "It's resentment. She was in the department when I came. She expected to be made assistant, but they gave the position to me."

"Are you being nice?" I snapped.

"No—natural."

I smiled then before I asked, "She seems to know a lot about Carl Briggs. Any special reason?"

"He liked women," she replied rather coolly.

"Just what did you hear in the washroom?" I asked, determined to know something definite about Eva Sutton.

"Mr. Doane will be waiting for you," she answered. I can take a hint even if it is as broad as a barn door. I turned away then without any further questions.

I wouldn't have blamed Beth a bit if she had resented me for the rest of her life. I was thinking about that and blaming myself for being an interfering old fool as I went through the drug and perfume department. A girl stepped out from behind a demonstration table and sprayed me with some vile-smelling perfume from an atomizer. I'm particular about perfumes and gave that girl an awful glare which froze her speech before she was half through. I heard her say something about "a frost-bitten old harridan" and I didn't blame her. After all, she was only doing her job even though she made me smell like a street-walker. I kept sniffing at myself, my nose going like a rabbit's, while I waited for Charlie. Smelling to high heaven makes you feel so self-conscious. I imagined everybody was looking at me. They probably were thinking I had Saint Vitus dance or some other affliction because of the twitching of my nose. Charlie didn't help matters any when he came down, took one sniff and said:

"Come up and sit in my office for a while, will you? It needs disinfecting."

I was in no humor to jest. I plunged into my reason for wanting to see him. He took the story about his father and Mrs. Briggs squarely. He hadn't known about it. There was no reason why he should. He just shook his head dubiously for a moment and then said, "Well, I suppose she was pretty once. It makes me feel better about the old man, though. I always thought he was a Sunday School superintendent and nothing else. I'm glad he did it. He never had much of a life. I used to pity him. When I was fresh out of college, with all the 'ologies running through my head, I thought the store was a substitute for the things I knew Father wasn't getting. Mother wasn't much of a wife to him."

Charlie is one of the few men I've known who has been able to see his mother clearly without sentiment. After all, mothers are women first and traditions afterward. He went on, "Dad leading a double life." He shook his head as if he still couldn't believe it. "You never can be sure of people, can you?"

"No, least of all a detective," I reminded him. "You're both in it. Why didn't you tell me that you had been making a spectacle of yourself over the girl?"

"I haven't done a thing except hang about in the jewelry department most of the time," he grinned at me.

"You did enough to have Peter suspect you both of murder. He'll develop a case of circumstantial evidence against you that may be your finish," I warned him.

"Gosh, that's bad!" He took hold of my arm and steered me off to one side. "You know, Ethel, that sort of lets me into it."

"What on earth are you talking about?" I had had all the riddles I wanted for one day.

I nearly collapsed when he told me. "I was down there this morning," he said as cool as you please.

"You what?" I couldn't believe my ears.

"Naturally I didn't say anything about it when the detective started asking questions. Neither did Herbert, for that matter."

"Herbert!" I exclaimed.

He nodded. He was thinking, so was I, and from his next remark I know we both had the same idea. He shook himself as if he would be rid of the thought and said, "But that's ridiculous."

"Is it?" I asked.

"Now, Ethel. You don't for one moment think—"

"I'll think anything I like," I snapped back at him. "Did Herbert see you?"

"No. That is—I don't think he did."

"Why not if you saw him?" I demanded.

"I didn't see him."

"Charlie, for heaven's sake, talk sense, will you? First you say you saw him, then you say you didn't. What are you talking about, anyhow?"

"I heard him," he answered, "over the partition."

"Tell me about it."

"I wanted to have a talk with Mrs. Briggs. I was going to suggest that she retire on a pension. She was a good buyer, I guess, but she couldn't get around and I figured she'd be better off out of the store. I had my little talk all prepared."

"You must have gone down the back way," I interrupted.

"I did," he replied. "Just as I was about to go into her office I heard Herbert's voice. They must have been having some sort of an argument, because Herbert sounded cross."

"Go on," I urged.

"I walked through one of the other offices and out by the narrow corridor to the side entrance."

"At what time?" I asked.

"Just before the store opened," he replied.

"Did any one see you?"

"I don't know. Say, you sound like your friend Conklin."

"I ought to, I've been with him all day. Charlie," I put a hand on his arm, "you must be careful. Why don't you tell Peter?"

"And spend the night in the hoosegow? No, thanks."

"You're sure Mrs. Briggs was alive when you heard Herbert speak?"

"Of course she was. I heard her voice."

"That's something, but not much," I agreed.

"It can't be important." He tried to brush the thought aside.

"Can't it? That's where you're mistaken. The person who killed Mrs. Briggs knew you were down there. How, I don't know unless he was in your father's little office peeking through the porthole. I'm sure he knows."

"Why are you so positive?"

"Did you call Beth and ask her to meet you in the office?"

"No," he answered promptly.

"Then you were framed. The murderer knew she would tell her reason for being there. What are we going to do?" I'm afraid I was close to the wailing-point just then. "When Peter learns about this he'll arrest you." My anxiety seemed to impress him just a little.

"There's something friend Peter doesn't know yet which may change his mind," he said grimly.

"I can't stand any more riddles. If you've anything to tell me, out with it," I insisted.

"Don't be obvious about it and don't look startled," he warned, "but take a good look at what's in my hand."

He moved up beside me and put his hand through my arm. His fist was closed. As we walked slowly he opened his fingers and I saw a few feathers nestling in his palm.

"What is it, a new trout fly?" I asked acidly. "I'm in no mood for trifling nonsense."

"It's a dart used by the natives down in the South Seas. They put them in blowguns and use them to kill things," he explained.

"Is it poisoned?" I asked. I knew that much about darts.

"They usually are."

"Where did you get it?"

"I brought it back with me."

"No, no, no," I said impatiently. "Where did it come from now. Was it blown at you?"

He laughed.

"You have a queer sense of humor," I said annoyed.

"Ethel sweetheart" (when he talks like that I'm putty in his hands), "you came within an ace of losing your most ardent admirer." He said it jocularly enough, but there was grim seriousness under the surface which I didn't miss.

"What do you mean?" I asked quickly.

"Some one in the store doesn't want me here. This cute little weapon was cleverly fixed into the pad on my chair. I sat on it."

I clutched at his arm, "Charlie, you don't mean they tried to kill you that way, do you? I never heard of any one being murdered in the seat."

He laughed uproariously for a moment and between chuckles said, "Killed in the pants." I hadn't meant to be funny. His eyes were moist from tears of laughter when he finally managed to say, "I'm afraid that was the idea. Those darts are supposed to be poisoned. I called them poison darts when I brought them in and hung the panel on the wall of my office."

"Fine idea of toys you have," I snorted.

Charlie then gave, to me, a perfect example of understatement, for he said in all seriousness, "You know, Ethel, things are beginning to be a bit complicated."

I laughed. I couldn't help myself. It was his turn to look hurt. "What are you going to do about it?" I asked.

"Nothing for the moment. Your friend Peter probably wouldn't believe me, anyhow."

I was wondering why he didn't say something about Beth. The news that she was married to Carl Briggs hadn't startled him as I thought it would. When he did mention her it was to ask, "Isn't she wonderful?"

"She's in a tight spot along with you. They electrocute women in this state, you know," I warned.

"You're crossing bridges before you come to them. Our job is to get the murderer. We know Peter Conklin is wrong."

"But why not tell him about the dart?" I insisted.

"I'm not telling any one but you."

"But—"

"Don't argue with me." He stopped my speech. "I want the person who fixed this thing in my chair to become uneasy. If you had planned a rather clever way to kill a man you would be uneasy until he was dead, wouldn't you?" he asked.

"I suppose so," I admitted.

"I don't want my embryo assassin to know that I've been warned. I'll be safe as long as he thinks the darts are poisonous. I want you to keep your eyes open. I'll do the same. Don't give me away."

"For heaven's sake, do be careful," I urged as he prepared to leave me.

"That goes for you, too. If I'm out of the way, you can't prove anything, but you might be a nuisance, so watch your step."

"I'll take care of myself," I assured him. "You're the one I'm worrying about. You act as if this were a tea-party. Beth Oliver's story about that telephone call—"

"Charming girl, by the way," he interrupted me.

"Charm, your granny!" I was annoyed. "Don't you see you're headed for the electric chair? Peter will find out about your being down there this morning. You didn't see any one. You have no alibi. Where were you from the time you left those offices until you reappeared there?"

"On the way back to my office."

"Who saw you?"

"No one that I remember. I used the private lift."

"Which is probably full of your fingerprints," I moaned. "You're a blind jackass, Charlie Doane, putting your head right into a noose."

"Aren't you being a little emotional for you, of all people?" he chided.

"I'm thinking about Peter Conklin. He's been baffled long enough. He's talking to the press representatives right now. Lord only knows what he's telling them. Can't you get it through your head that he suspects you?"

"But he has nothing tangible," he objected.

"He doesn't need anything tangible. Suppose they find your fingerprints in that lift?"

"I was in it, why not?"

"Heavens above!" I exclaimed. "A man certainly can be dumb and exasperating without half trying. When Peter found you in that room you were wearing gloves, weren't you?" I didn't wait for him to answer. "How are you going to explain your fingerprints? You didn't make them when you had your gloves on. He'll ask you questions. He's bound to arrest you."

"I can just say I used the lift sometime during the morning."

"And make things that much worse for yourself. He'll think you were in there listening to what was being said."

"But I can prove my story, if necessary, by Herbert." He positively beamed at me as if the thing were all settled.

"Herbert has his own neck to worry about," I reminded him. "You tell your story and then what happens? Herbert admits being in there talking to her, but don't forget he didn't see you. Herbert will say the woman was alive when he left her. You can't prove that you left that suite of offices before the crime was committed. No one saw you leave. You can't account for your time. O dear!" I was frightfully upset at the prospect before us.

"There's the dart," he offered. I think he began to wonder just what would happen to him.

"You could have put the dart there yourself. It's too thin." Then I said a silly thing. "Of course, if you had died from the dart—" I was so serious that his sudden burst of laughter both startled and annoyed me. Then I, too, saw how funny it was and laughed with him. A good laugh does things for you. We both felt less afraid.

We were in a jam and knew it. Peter would be furious and doubly suspicious when he learned that Charlie and Herbert had been in those little offices that morning. I was trying to think of some plan, when Charlie said very quietly,

"I think I have the answer to our immediate problem."

"What is it?" I asked eagerly.

"You're working with Peter Conklin," he replied; "it wouldn't be fair to tell you. Go back there and see him. Pick up what information you can, but keep still about this. I'll have to work fast." He took my elbow and steered me back across the main floor.

We went through the jewelry and book departments. He left me at the little door. At that moment I had an idea. I clutched at his sleeve and held him fast. He's a tall thing and I had to stretch up on my toes to whisper to him.

"Willie will tell Peter that he saw you and Herbert. Had you thought of that?"

"Yes," he answered, "I've thought of that, but perhaps Willie won't be found."

I released my grasp on his arm. He left me standing there. I'm sure my mouth was hanging open. I hadn't thought much about Willie one way or another. Where was he? What had happened to him? I knew Peter was concerned about him and annoyed because he hadn't been located all day.

As I went into the little corridor and walked to the office which Peter had been using I tried to fathom Charlie's meaning. There was a threat under his words and I didn't like it. I was to like it less during the next hour or two and I must admit now that my faith was put on the rack and almost torn to shreds.

# CHAPTER TWELVE

While waiting for Peter I had a nice chat with Davis. He, above all things, confided in me that he wanted to be a writer. Perhaps if I had not had that confidence this story would never have been written. He has been of inestimable help to me with his notes, memories and suggestions. We are doing this on a fifty-fifty basis. If he can get a little money ahead he says he will give up his job as a stenographer and do nothing but write. My first impulse was to endow him with enough money to last him a year and let him see what he could do. I discarded that notion because a man should work for the thing he wants. I can help him if he gets in a tight spot.

Peter came back a little refreshed, I thought, after his interview with the representatives of the press. He said he gave them the story of the first two murders and nothing else. He kept his suspicions to himself, thank fortune. The reporters were pleased with the story of Mrs. Doyle and promised to run it on the first page in a little square box. Peter said that all police cars had been advised to look out for her, as well as all rounds-men and traffic officers. He explained to me that the call had gone out from headquarters to every precinct in the city.

"This would have been unnecessary," he said scathingly, "if you had taken her address."

It was then that I remembered that her address was in the store because of the statue she was having sent home. Strange how we can forget the obvious thing until unexpectedly we are forced to remember. Peter gave me a nasty look for the second time that day when I told him.

"What's the matter," he asked, "losing your pep?"

I ignored that remark and waited while he sent Davis out to find Smith, who was to put the wheels in motion to get at Mrs. Doyle's address. Before Davis went on his errand he pointed to some reports which had been waiting for Peter's attention. They had to do with the last crime. Peter read them quickly and gave me a summary.

A gun had been found at the bottom of the elevator shaft. It was free of fingerprints. Further investigation proved that it had been taken from stock in the sporting goods section. The clerk in the department told them, when asked, that Charlie Doane had been up there the night before looking at fishing tackle and guns.

Peter was too satisfied with the report to suit me. "You see," he said, "how the net begins to close in once you get on the right track?"

"You remind me of the native who when asked if he didn't think Bryce Canyon a beautiful spot replied, 'I dunno about its beauty, but I'll say this for it. It's an awful place to lose a cow.'"

Peter laughed and replied, "They say faith moves mountains and you sure have it. On the other hand, I'm supposed to be a detective and being suspicious is part of my job. I'm going to do a little investigating that you won't like. Can you occupy yourself for an hour or two?"

I sniffed at that as we waited for Smith to return with Mrs. Doyle's address. We had a discussion about her. Smith was doubtful about Mrs. Doyle. He didn't believe she'd come without a warrant.

"Let me go for her," I suggested. "She'll come for me, I'm sure. I'll call my chauffeur. He'll be here in fifteen minutes."

"Detail Carter to ride to the Bronx with Miss Thomas," Peter instructed Smith; and explained to me, "An officer with you will save time."

After I put the call through for Malcolm and the car, Peter called the store operator and told her to find Charlie for him. I could hear the signal bonging out in the store. Charlie's call was one long and two short bongs. After a minute or so the operator reported that she was unable to locate Charlie. Peter turned to me as if it were my fault.

"If you don't find him before, he'll be in his office after five-thirty. We're to have a meeting," I told him.

"I hope so," he replied. From the reproachful looks he cast in my direction you'd think I had Charlie tucked away in my sleeve somewhere.

"Why don't you go on with your investigation and prove yourself wrong, so you can get on the right track?" I asked. "Charlie Doane isn't the murderer and the sooner you're sure of it the better."

"Then who is?" he demanded.

"Haven't you any other clues?" I asked innocently enough I thought.

"Clues!" he bellowed. "Clues! Sure I have, and they all point to your precious Charlie!" He faced me indignantly. "That private elevator is full of his fingerprints and yet he was wearing gloves when we discovered him in that little room."

"Gentlemen usually wear gloves when they are on the street," I reminded him.

"I'm not talking about gentlemen. I'm talking about murderers," he barked. "How and when did his fingerprints get there?"

I could have answered that question then, but I didn't I try to wait for my bridges before I go over them.

"And what's more," Peter railed at my silence, "when he opened that little porthole with his gloves on he wiped all fingerprints off."

"He could have, but he didn't and you know it. He merely opened the window to show it to us. When you've exhausted him, I'd begin working on Eva Sutton, if I were you."

"She's just a dizzy blonde scared out of her wits." (His tone said clearly, "Why bother me with that now?") "What have you got against her, anyhow?"

"She's clever, smarter than we realize," I argued. "When you know why she's afraid, you'll have some of the answer to your riddle."

"She'll just pull the noose tight about the necks of

your friends."

"She tried that," I insisted. "She didn't explain her fear to us. She evaded the question and centered your interest on first Robert Doane and Mrs. Briggs and then on Charlie and Beth Oliver. She fooled us both, at the time."

"More of your intuition?" he asked mockingly. "I'll try my system for a while."

He left then. I've no idea why he was so stubborn and I've never asked him. It does no good to remind a man that he was wrong. The woman who says to a man "I told you so," is nothing short of a fool.

My mind had been full of murder all day. I knew Charlie Doane was not the murdering type, but Peter didn't. I tried to fit the pieces of the puzzle together as I went out into the wide corridor. I met Grover in the hall. He asked me if I had seen Peter. He seemed very serious and intent. I left him and walked to the receiving-room, when the idea struck me. What had Charlie meant when he said Willie Evans wouldn't be found?

I stopped at the desk and asked the man who was taking Willie's place what he knew about Willie's habits. When I learned that Willie usually ate his lunch somewhere in the nether regions I extracted full information and decided on a little investigation of my own. I took the elevator as directed down one floor. It was a bit bewildering down there, but I finally found the room and the man in charge. There were boxes on wheels called wheelers, full of refuse and trash, and over at one side a chute into which the man dumped the papers, etc.

The attendant was just emptying a wheeler into the chute as I coughed to attract his attention. He was surprised.

"Are you in charge here?" I asked.

The man was curious and nodded.

"Did you know Willie Evans?" I went on.

"Sure," the man answered.

"See him to-day?"

"For a few minutes," the man replied.

"Tell me about it."

"What's the matter with him?" the man asked anxiously.

"I'll tell you that later. When did you see Evans?"

"He came down here this morning to eat his lunch. He came every day," the man explained. "He kept an eye on this place for me while I went out to get some coffee."

"Then you left him here this morning?"

"Yeah. He came down like he always did and said hell was popping upstairs. We chatted for a few minutes. He sat on that box right over there and began to eat his sandwiches." He pointed to the box worn shiny, undoubtedly by a succession of Willies who had sat upon it. I controlled a shudder. It was a dull dreary place to eat one's lunch.

"Were you alone when Willie came down?"

"Yes, ma'am," he replied.

"You're sure of that?" I insisted.

"Yup."

"Where did Willie go from here?" was my next question.

"Gosh, I dunno. He could have got me in Dutch, him leaving me flat the way he did. I'm not supposed to be away. You see, Willie always covered me," he explained.

"What did Willie tell you about the things that had been happening upstairs?"

"He told me about Mrs. Briggs, that was all. He said the police were up there bothering everybody."

"Did he advance any theories about the murder?" I asked hopefully.

"I dunno as you'd call it a theory, but Willie said that son of hers would probably be in bad because he had been in there this morning."

I was excited. Perhaps I would find the clue we needed. "Did he mention any one else?"

"Nope." He thought for a moment. "No, he didn't."

"I'm afraid your friend Willie has been murdered," I

said seriously.

"Quit your kidding, lady." The man laughed in my face. "Who'd want to murder him?" There was contempt in the question.

"That's what I'm trying to find out," I replied. "When you came back and found Willie gone, think hard," I cautioned, "did you notice anything unusual about the place?"

"No," he said after a moment's thoughtful consideration, "unless leaving his lunch half finished would be unusual. I thought he'd be back any minute. Willie loved to eat. He was sort of a glutton. When he didn't come back I folded his lunch in his paper and put it up there." He pointed to a shelf and a grease-stained paper parcel.

"Was there any sign of a struggle?" I asked.

"I didn't notice none. I try to keep the place clean, but there's usually some paper and trash scattered around. I just swept up a minute ago," he said with pride.

"Everything was as you left it when you returned?" I was insistent on that point.

"Except Willie was gone," he said promptly. "Say, wait a minute. I left a wheeler right there by the chute. Willie must have emptied it, because it was moved back."

"Did Willie do your work for you, too?" I asked.

"Sometimes if the wheelers came down too fast he'd empty them."

"Where does the chute lead?"

"To the baler downstairs."

"How do you get there?"

The man's face went white. "Say, you don't think—"

"I'm not thinking and don't you, if you're wise," I cautioned. "Just tell me how to get down there."

I went back to the elevator, following his instructions, and down one more flight. I was in the sub-basement. I had never seen the underside of a big building before. I have always accepted their warmth and air-cooling systems without thinking about them. There was a furnace room near the elevator, the door of which was open. Great asbestos-covered pipes ran in all directions. Square tin conveyors paralleled them in many places. I went down a long corridor which was beside the shafts of store elevators. The counterweights and wires rattled and groaned as somewhere above the cars started and stopped. There was a dank damp smell. Escaping steam hissed from some of the pipes. It was a clammy place. I expected to see spiders and crawly things any moment, but I didn't.

I hurried. I didn't like the place at all. At last I found the room where a tall blond Swede was in charge. He introduced me to the baling machine. I can remember letter-presses in my father's office years ago. The baler looked like a huge and more elaborate press.

The blond Swede was not surprised to see me. I can rather imagine the conversation which was carried on through the chute after I had left the room above.

At that moment a rush of paper, cardboard, broken boxes and other rubbish slid down the chute into the baler.

"Does that come from upstairs?" I asked.

"Yes, ma'am."

"How large is a bale?"

He showed me one which was standing at one side. I shuddered. It was large enough to hold the body of a man. The thought was too horrible and I tried to control my racing mind, but it was no use. Pictures of horror floated before my eyes. I fought them hopelessly. I imagine a person trying to escape insanity must feel as I felt then. It couldn't be. I was letting my mind play with something which was too inhuman and too ghastly, and yet—

"How many bales do you make during a day?" I asked as I struggled toward normalcy.

"That depends," he answered.

"On what?"

"The amount of rubbish that comes down. I had six yesterday afternoon and this morning."

"Where are they?"

"Zuccini calls for them every day about one o'clock. We can't keep them here, they take up too much room," he explained.

"When did you take that one out of the machine?" I pointed to the bale he had just shown me.

"About a half-hour ago," he replied.

"Did you bale anything between ten and twelve?" I asked.

"Yes, ma'am, I did."

"And Mr. Zuccini now has it?"

"Yes, ma'am."

"Where can I find this Zuccini person?"

He gave me the address. It was in the Italian district downtown—that colorful and smelly fringe of Greenwich Village.

I hurried out of the place, anxious to leave my horrible thoughts behind me, but I was unsuccessful. I would have told Peter of my suspicions had he been in the office, but he wasn't there. His man Carter, however, was waiting for me. Malcolm was very superior when Carter and I approached the door. I gave Malcolm the address of Zuccini and I noticed his nose go up.

"I thought we were going to the Bronx," Carter remarked.

"We are, but we're going downtown first," I answered without explaining.

"Okay," Carter said as he slid into the seat next to Malcolm. "Step on it, big boy. I'll take care of you." Malcolm made no reply.

Once away from the store I began to enjoy myself after a fashion. As we threaded our way through the narrow, smelling, congested streets, I knew Malcolm was loathing the experience. He turned once and asked, "Are you sure, madam?"

He finally stopped the car in front of a combination residence and warehouse. As he held the door for me a hundred curious children, attracted by the policeman, gathered about the car. Malcolm did his best to shoo them off. A large overripe woman, a baby in her arms, suspiciously blocked the door to the house. She looked like a Neapolitan. I tried my Italian on her. It worked. Her face broke into an immediate smile as I rapidly explained my errand. We had a nice but short conversation while she sent one of the children in search of her husband, who was somewhere down the street. He was excited as I told him what I wanted.

Carter and Malcolm, being in the dark and curious about the rapid flow of Italian, drew together for the first time since we started the trip downtown.

"Si, si, Signora," Zuccini said; "this way, please." He led us through a long covered way into his warehouse, where great bales of paper were stored.

He remembered the ones he had brought back from Doane's and with the help of a swarthy, wiry young man with sullen brooding eyes, who miraculously appeared from somewhere, they began moving the bales.

It was the young man who drew away from one of the bales with a horrified look at his hand. He explained to Zuccini that the bale felt sticky.

"What are you after?" Carter finally asked, unable to hold his curiosity any longer.

"I think there's a man in there," I replied. Both Carter and Malcolm were aghast.

"Open it up!" Carter ordered Zuccini.

Zuccini took a heavy pair of wire-cutters.

"I wouldn't look if I were you," Carter cautioned. There was the snip of shears and a snapping report as one of the wires broke.

"I don't know what you expect, but it may be a nasty sight," Malcolm suggested, a warning in his voice.

The wires were off. Zuccini and the young man, with flat forks, began to loosen the tightly packed paper.

"You beat anything I ever saw," Carter said as, fascinated, I watched the men pulling off layer after layer, getting nearer to the spot which the young man had so adequately described as sticky. I'll never criticize people again for their morbid curiosity. I could no more have stopped watching them than I could have taken wing the next moment, though the sensation I had at the pit of my stomach for a second was as near to flying as I'll ever come. I've done everything else that people do and a few things they don't seem to have thought of—that is, generally speaking, of course—but I still stick to terra firma. The air may be safe and I'll believe all they tell me about air miles and the comparative safety of flying as opposed to any other form of travel, but I'll continue to take a train when I want to travel. Each time I've been tempted to fly something horrible makes me more determined than ever to stay on the ground. First it was Rockne and then that most beloved of all Americans, Will Rogers and his friend Wiley Post. No, sir! I'm going to stay right here on the ground.

As layer after layer came off, the men worked more gingerly. I saw the assistant turn suddenly white as the flat fork he was using hit an obstruction. Zuccini peered into the bale and turned pallid. I saw a smeared hand for a fleeting moment and closed my eyes just as the assistant was taken violently ill. Poor chap, I felt sorry for him. I kept my eyes closed and tried to hang onto myself. Stars, moons, crescents and bars of light danced before my eyes as I heard Carter and Zuccini talking over the assistant's noises.

"Who is it?" I heard Carter ask.

"I can't tell yet," Zuccini's voice answered. There was more rustling of paper, which sounded weird and uncanny in the dark space within which I held myself with my tightly closed eyes.

"Couldn't you tell there was some one in it?" Carter asked as the work went on.

"No. You wouldn't know," Zuccini's voice answered. "They are very heavy, these bales."

That picture was too horrible for my imagination. I felt myself swaying, but I wouldn't call to Malcolm. He had warned me and I had been contrary enough to look. I'd have given a hundred dollars for some good strong smelling-salts right then. I tried to move away from that awful thing, still afraid to open my eyes. I bumped into something, there was a crash which frightened me half out of my wits. I stepped on broken glass and had to open my eyes.

"The poor devil." It was Carter's voice ringing in my ears as I stumbled away from that room into a narrow hall which led toward the street.

I've done the Eden Musee and the wax works in London, but never in my life have I seen anything as horrible as that one smeared hand which for a single instant the assistant raised from the mass of paper on his flat fork.

# CHAPTER THIRTEEN

I've scoffed at a good many things in my time and most of them, I must admit, have been phenomena I did not understand—which is, I suppose, a human weakness. I've read in books and the papers stories of and about fiends and have always maintained an aloof and skeptical point of view. My skepticism deserted me.

As I raced along that alley I was not only fleeing from the gruesome thing we had found there, but was also trying to escape an idea which had been forming in my mind. There was a fiend at large, lurking, ready to pounce, no one knew when or where. Emotional peaks are not maintained for very long, however, and my haste dispelled some of my terror. When I reached the end of the passage I was faced by a new problem. I was lost. I decided to wait where I was until the others came.

I knew I had acted like a frightened schoolgirl. I was wondering what Carter and Malcolm would think of me as I stopped. Conveniently at hand was what I believe is known in plumbing parlance as an elbow. Anyhow, it was a large asbestos-covered pipe which offered me a place to sit and compose myself. I was a mass of quivers inside and my thoughts were just about as chaotic. I took a cigarette out of my bag, lit it and mentally snubbed my nose at the "No Smoking" sign which hung almost directly in front of me.

Smoking may be just a habit, a nervous expression or an emotional outlet of some kind. I don't know anything about that, but I wouldn't have taken fifty dollars for that cigarette at that moment. It calmed me. I inhaled it deeply and let the smoke trickle slowly from my nostrils. It normalized me as nothing else could have done and my thoughts began to regiment themselves properly.

There was no question in my mind about the murderer. As I sat there, my thin thread of smoke caught by unseen drafts, vanishing over my head, I knew we had been on the wrong track all day. There was a fiend at large in the Doane store. A madman killing either for the sheer lust of it or else prompted by an unreasonable fear. His reason was not important. He must be stopped before more damage was done. No one but a fiend incarnate would have done what had been done during the day at Doane's.

I kept asking myself the everlasting and eternal why. What had Mrs. Briggs discovered that made her death imperative? How was Carl Briggs connected with that discovery—and Charlie, what of him? Why had an attempt been made on his life? I've always found that once your mind accepts an idea you are caught by it and can't think clearly or rationally of anything else until that idea is settled one way or another. I didn't believe that Mrs. Briggs' affair with Robert Doane had anything to do with the murders. I knew it was something else, it had to be; and yet my mind nibbled at the idea like a mouse gnawing at a cheese. I couldn't get away from Mrs. Briggs, her son, Beth and Charlie.

I tried a new method of approach. There have been a few times in my life when on the spur of the moment I could have easily committed murder. I suppose we all have those periods of intense burning rage. We wouldn't be human if we didn't. That, I think, is understandable; but the commission of crime after crime, such ruthless killing, was something my mind could not fathom. I've never been particularly religious, that being an emotional outlet I didn't need because I've always been so busy with other things, but I had had a religion as all of us do. Emerson's "Essay on Compensation" has been a Bible and a manual of action for me.

I don't know why I thought of Emerson as I perched myself on that piece of pipe and smoked one cigarette after another, waiting for the others. I wasn't thinking of compensation particularly, but it did seem to me that there should be some proportion between the motive and the crimes committed. What did the fiend fear? What price would he have to pay if discovered? It had to be something very important in one's own eyes at least to make a person kill as this one had killed that day. What situation in the store could explain it? It had to be important, since Charlie was involved.

I looked at my watch. It was nearly four. Heavens! There was so much to be done. I had a trip to the Bronx ahead of me. Peter must be notified of my discovery. I felt horribly pressed for time. I wanted to do something at once which would effectively stop the murderer. But what? Right there I made my greatest mistake. If I had gone on thinking instead of worrying about things I'm sure I could have spared another life. I was so intent upon the necessity of immediate action that the obviousness of a precautionary move did not occur to me until it was too late.

My actions were prompted by an unknown and unseen fear. I think I can truthfully say that up to that moment the only thing I really ever feared was a skidding automobile because of the helplessness one feels in such a situation. I wanted to be doing things.

The sound of footsteps coming toward me was reassuring. It was Malcolm, looking a bit peaked in the dim light of the passage.

"The officer will stay here," he said, "and requests that you notify a Mr. Conklin of what has happened."

His stiff propriety did things for me. Good old Malcolm!

"Come along. They may have a telephone in the house," I suggested as I stood up.

"Your back's all white," he said and began brushing me with the flat of his hand.

It's a curious thing the way your mind will turn to trivial things when you think you're completely absorbed in something big and important. I really didn't care how I looked at the moment, and yet I did appreciate Malcolm's thoughtful gesture—any woman would.

The Zuccinis did have a telephone and the rotund woman with the baby waited and listened as I talked to Peter. "I've found Willie Evans," I announced.

"Where was he, tucked under Mrs. Doyle's arm?" he asked facetiously.

The balance of my story took all the humor out of Peter. "I'll send men down. What are you going to do?" he asked.

"Get Mrs. Doyle and be back at the store in time for the meeting," I promised.

"You'll have to go some. I can send a man up for her," he suggested.

"No," I replied. "I'd rather go myself. I need some air after what has happened."

"Tell your chauffeur to pick up a motorcycle officer at Twenty-third Street and the Express Highway," he suggested. "I'll telephone instructions."

Malcolm was not too interested in the motorcycle officer who was to be our escort. He did, however, go over to the Express Highway, which saves a great deal of time when one is going uptown. As Malcolm slowed down on the curve at Twenty-third Street we picked up the waiting officer, a trim Mercury on a motorcycle. It was a thrilling experience for me. The policeman on his giddy machine with siren wide open cleared the way for us as we raced uptown, hit Riverside Drive and shot north to One Hundred Thirty-fifth Street. Then we had a mad ride across town, missing death by inches several times as Malcolm, intent but disliking his job, followed the trail blazed by the officer.

Mrs. Doyle was having a cup of tea when I arrived. She poured me a cup. It was strong, a first cousin to lye, but I was glad to have it as I tried to convince her that she was duty bound to return to the store with me. Her daughter, a pleasant girl who was nicely dressed, took sides with me and we were finally able to persuade her.

As we left her house she said to her daughter, "Mind now, call Denny at five-thirty and give him a good supper. He's me youngest," she explained to me, "and works nights."

It was after five when we left the Doyle flat and as we wove our way downtown the afternoon traffic became very heavy. We made good time, however, until we started across town and then not even the shrieking siren could move us through some of the cross streets at better than a snail's pace.

Mrs. Doyle talked, asking me what she could possibly know that would help the detective. I told her my theory.

"I did see a man," she said. "He bumped into me."

"What did he look like?" I asked eagerly. "Can you describe him?"

"Sure. He was wearing a gray suit," she answered.

"But his face," I urged, waiting expectantly.

"Now, how could I see his face?" she asked. "Me bent over trying to fix me garter and him bumping into me and nearly knocking me down. I was that mad," she said.

"But wasn't there some one thing about him which you could recognize?" I insisted.

"He was going through the door I had used when I looked up," she answered, "and it was just the back of him I saw. I just saw something gray for a minute and he was gone."

It was something, but not much, and I hoped that Peter would be able to make more out of it than I could.

At about twenty minutes of six we pulled into the Doane side drive and found the doors locked, as of course we would, since the store closes at five. We walked down to the door of the receiving-room and into the little offices where Peter was waiting for us.

"Smart work, Mrs. Sherlock Holmes," he greeted me. "Now if you'll just find Charlie Doane for me, everything will be all right."

"Charlie?" I gasped. "What do you mean?"

"He's vanished. Can't find him anywhere and he's taken the Oliver girl with him."

"Then he's hiding," I said.

"I sort of had the same idea myself," Peter replied sarcastically.

"No, no. You don't understand." I told him then about the dart fixed in the seat of Charlie's chair, while Mrs. Doyle stood by, eyes agape.

"Why didn't you tell me this before?" he demanded angrily.

"Because he told me to keep it a secret," I flared back. I was tired and thought Peter was unreasonable.

"There's too many secrets in this place," he said scornfully and turned to Mrs. Doyle.

She repeated what she had told me coming down in the car. I sat back and listened and smoked one of Davis' cigarettes. The store was very quiet and, except for a few lights, dimly lit.

You know how your eyes rove as you sit thinking and doing nothing. I saw that little whispering window and was thinking about the part it had played in the day's tragedies. It was open.

As I look back on it now, much of what happened might have been averted. That is, I think so, but one never knows, because hindsight is so much more accurate than foresight ever can be. Then, too, there is this to be said for Peter and all of us connected with the crimes— there was very little time for thinking. Events piled themselves one upon the other too rapidly for any one of us connected with the store to be able to stand off and get any sort of perspective. Peter had one crime to solve and before his routine with that case had been completed he had another murder on his hands, a much more daring one than the first. The day had raced away from us with breathless rapidity.

"Do you think you could identify the man by the suit he wore?" I heard Peter ask.

"I think so," Mrs. Doyle answered.

It was then that I believe I innocently signed a death-warrant for another person. I don't know. They never quite determined when she died. Peter has tried to convince me that the poor thing was probably dead at the time I spoke. It came to me suddenly. "Peter," I said, interrupting him, "why didn't we think of it before?"

"What?" he asked, annoyed.

"Eva Sutton and Carl Briggs were in the receiving-room. Willie was there, too. Carl Briggs is dead. Willie is dead. I'll bet Eva Sutton knows who was in these offices this morning just about nine o'clock. That's the thing which has terrified her," I finished, quite sure that I was right.

"Maybe," he admitted thoughtfully. "If we can make her talk and Mrs. Doyle here can identify the same man we have our case clinched." He looked at Mrs. Doyle for a moment. "I want you to identify the man on your own before we get Eva Sutton to talk." He turned to me. "How about that meeting? Is it still on?"

For an answer I took the telephone and called the executive offices. Herbert's secretary said he was waiting for a meeting. I told the girl to tell him we would be up immediately.

"Good," Peter said. "The man who has been doing these things knows this store inside and out, upside and down." He turned to Davis, "Get the Sutton girl, will you?"

As he was giving Mrs. Doyle her instructions, I crossed the room intent on the small ash-tray piled high with cigarette stubs sitting at Davis' elbow. Why are men so sloppy about ashes? I smoke, but when an ash-tray is full I empty it into a waste-basket—that's what they are for. Davis offered me a cigarette as he prepared to go on his errand, but before I accepted a light I lifted that brimming tray gingerly and with a sniff of disgust which made him laugh, dumped it into the waste-basket.

During this little housewifely job of mine Peter had said to Mrs. Doyle, "When we go upstairs, you are to sit outside and wait for us. I want you to take a good look at every man who passes you as we come out."

As I smoked I looked up at the whispering window. It was nearly closed. I cocked my head from one side to the other and even went back to the chair in which I had been sitting a few minutes before, to make sure. I thought the window had been open. The others paid no attention to me and I decided that it was just a shadow, after all, which had played tricks with me.

Davis returned and reported Eva Sutton had left the department after the store closed. The policeman who had been hovering about her all day for protection said she had gone to the executive offices.

"We'll probably find her up there," Peter said.

Just as we were ready to start for the sixth floor Mrs. Curtis, who had had no use of her office at all that day, appeared.

"We'll be out of your way soon," Peter said as he recognized her.

"As long as I can have my office to-night it will be all right," she replied. "I really came to check with you about the chalice and the rosary beads."

"Why?" Peter asked, surprised.

"Because I'm responsible for them. They belong to my department. If you're going to hold them, I'll have to make out a memorandum to keep my figures straight."

"What was Mrs. Briggs doing with them?" I was wondering about that myself and was glad he asked the question.

"She borrowed them for a display she had made. The window came out last night. They should have been returned to me this morning," she explained.

"We'll have to hold them as evidence, so make whatever notes you need to cover yourself," Peter advised.

Mrs. Curtis went to her desk, pulled out a drawer, rooted in a mass of pads until she found one which would make a carbon copy, then bent over to make her notation. "Will you sign this?" Mrs. Curtis handed Peter the pad. Like a wise man he took a moment to read it before he signed.

As she was ready to leave, Peter said, "Mrs. Curtis, I wish you had been in your office this morning."

"I'm rather glad I wasn't. I'm still fond of life," she said with a grim conviction.

"It's so strange," Peter went on, "that in this store surrounded by hundreds, the murderer could make such a clean getaway."

"With each man and woman intent on his job, it's not so strange—that is if you know anything about department stores," Mrs. Curtis replied. "I was busy in the department, there's always so much to do on a Sales Day, and when I looked up and saw Mr. Doane going up the balcony stairs I was glad he was not his father."

I caught my breath. I knew what was coming. I saw a gleam grow in Peter's eye. It's curious how often an innocent conversation can get a person into trouble. Peter did it cleverly. I'm sure Mrs. Curtis had no idea that Peter was suspecting Charlie.

"That was before the store opened, wasn't it?" he asked.

She took the bait very neatly.

"A little before the opening bell." She went on to elaborate, "He went up the balcony steps and paused for a moment before he went into the private office. His father always stood in that spot and spoke to the employees every morning."

"Yes, we've heard about that," Peter said with keen satisfaction.

I wasn't conscious of Mrs. Curtis' leaving. I was busy thinking. If Charlie paused there and looked over the store, where was Herbert at that moment? Charlie told me he had heard but not seen Herbert. Where had Herbert gone?

I knew Peter would be furious again, but I had to tell him what I knew of Charlie's visit to the offices that morning and Herbert's possible part in the murder. He boiled over and gave me a good piece of his mind, but like all rows it did sort of clear the air.

"And I thought you were a clever woman," he said after his spontaneous anger had worn itself out.

I've never had any one say anything to me that was more scathing. I hadn't failed Peter really. His idea of me had failed him, but I felt sorry for him nevertheless, because he had tried me in the scales and I had been found wanting.

"We must find them," I urged.

"If it isn't too late."

They say misery loves company and his speech did confirm my fears, but that wasn't what I wanted at the time. "Peter, do you suppose—"

"We can suppose anything," he cut me short. "If Doane believed that we wouldn't find Willie, there must have been some idea at work in his mind. He knew Hastings was in here. He paused at the head of the stairs. I wonder what he saw, standing there?"

Peter pondered a minute and then asked, "If Doane saw anything which would have incriminated his brother-in-law, do you think he would have told me?"

"Not unless he was sure," I replied honestly.

"Perhaps he saw Herbert Hastings going toward the rear elevators early this morning. The build-up of events may have made him suspicious. I wish we knew what he knew," Peter went on with his puzzling.

"I don't know what it is that Beth Oliver has to tell me, but whatever it is, it must have some bearing on the case," I suggested.

"We don't know what they may have said to each other while they were having their luncheon," he said speculatively.

"You mean they might have been overheard?" I asked, for I wanted to know exactly what Peter was thinking.

He nodded and I felt that he was going to shut me out of the further developments of the case. We neither of us knew that I was to be mixed up in the awful business right to the very end.

I looked at my watch. It was exactly six o'clock. "I

must go," I said. "We were to have a meeting at five-thirty about store business. I'm late."

"Will they hold it without Doane?" he asked.

"I'll try it, at any rate. If Charlie is alive he'll be there," I said hopefully. "Besides, I told Herbert I was on my way."

"I'll go with you. I want to see Mr. Hastings. Don't let any one know that we've been looking for Mr. Doane and Miss Oliver. People sometimes give themselves away."

With Mrs. Doyle in tow we started for the sixth floor.

# CHAPTER FOURTEEN

On the sixth floor Herbert was pacing up and down the little railed enclosure which formed an anteroom for the executive offices. We put Mrs. Doyle into an easy-chair and went forward.

"I'm ready for the meeting," I said.

"This is no time for a meeting," he growled.

"It's the very time for it. Call your people together and let's get going." Bulldozing Herbert had always been easy for me.

"Where's Charlie?" he asked. "Wasn't he with you?"

"He'll be here," I said with more assurance than I felt. There was a lump in my throat which choked back my words as I tried to talk.

"I've been trying to find him for the last hour," he grumbled.

"He must be in the store somewhere," Peter suggested.

"I hope so." Herbert was either a genuine actor or else he really was afraid.

I had no idea what was in Peter's mind as we followed Herbert to his office. He was planning something, however. I could tell that by the expression of his eyes, which had grown more calculating than usual.

Herbert's office was impressive, with its somber massive furniture and morgue-like dimness. I've often wondered why men select and furnish their offices as they do. Why make the place in which you spend most of your life a drab horror? I've seen one or two business offices of which I approved. One was a little too ornate, done in the Empire tradition, but it was cheerful. The other was done in maple, looked clean and cheerful and would have been a pleasant place to work for any one at any time.

"I'll get the others," Herbert said as we settled ourselves in the deep leather chairs.

"Better get Banter, Kramer and Sandy McLeod, too," Peter requested.

"This is supposed to be a stockholders' meeting," Herbert objected, "between Grover, Doane, Miss Thomas and myself."

"I'm aware of that," Peter replied coldly. "I have no desire to interfere with your meeting, but I'd like to have you all together for a few minutes first. I've made a discovery which will interest all of you."

Herbert gave instructions to his secretary and we waited. I lit a cigarette and offered one to Peter, who refused. Herbert dragged one of those silly heavy ornate smoking-stands within my reach. I was interested in watching the people as they arrived one by one. There was speculation in their eyes as they trooped in and stood about uncomfortably, waiting for they knew not what. Each time the door opened or whenever I heard a commotion outside I looked up, hoping to see Charlie, but he did not appear. In the full course of his life I had never known Charlie to make a promise which he did not keep. He was never late for appointments, which fact was a close bond between us. He had jokingly promised me a drink after five o'clock. I suppose it was silly of me to be thinking about that, but I couldn't help myself. It wasn't that I wanted the drink, though I could have used it well enough. I was thinking of it as a promise which Charlie had failed to fulfil.

At Herbert's suggestion, after Grover, Banter, Kramer and Sandy had all arrived we went into the board-room, another of those massively furnished dark rooms with a long heavy table and great carved chairs too heavy for even a strong man to move with comfort. The atmosphere of the place had a deadening effect. You felt that you shouldn't speak above a whisper, and that was why Peter's voice was so startling when he began.

"I have found Willie Evans," he pronounced, and

paused, eying them carefully.

I saw nothing but the natural surprise that one could reasonably expect.

"Where?" Kramer asked.

"In a bale of waste-paper which had been taken out of the building," he replied.

Herbert looked sick, and no wonder. The implications in Peter's cold hard voice could not be ignored.

The others asked questions all at once. Peter explained about Willie Evans as briefly as possible. When he had finished there was a glum uneasy silence, broken by Peter's voice as he turned to Kramer.

"Where is Eva Sutton?" Peter demanded.

Kramer looked dumber than usual.

"I talked to her shortly after the store closed," Herbert said. "Isn't she in the department? She told me she was going to work to-night."

"She left to come up here. She hasn't been seen since," Peter answered. "How long did she stay here?" He turned to Herbert.

"I don't know exactly. Twenty minutes, perhaps longer."

"Can't you be sure, Mr. Hastings?" There was an insinuation in Peter's voice.

"No, not exactly." Herbert flushed as he replied.

Peter turned to Banter. "How long has Eva Sutton been employed in the store?"

Banter looked about the room for a moment and then said, "A year or more. I can give you the exact figures if you'd like me to look it up."

"Know anything about her?" Peter asked.

"She's been a very efficient clerk," Banter replied.

"How about her private life?" Peter asked.

Banter hesitated again. I was all agog. What had Peter unearthed that I knew nothing about? It sounded like the beginning of a good bit of rather juicy scandal and I know of few women who don't relish a bit of gossip every so often.

"I don't intend to drag the information out of you," Peter warned. "Eva Sutton lives in an apartment which is far beyond her means as an employee of this store. Which of the store executives is interested in Eva Sutton?"

"No one in particular," Banter began an evasion; "she is generally well liked."

"Do you mean to sit there and tell me that you don't know what is going on in the store?" Peter accused. "It's part of your job to know. Isn't it true that Eva Sutton is a particular friend of Mr. Hastings'?"

I was flabbergasted. So Herbert was leading a double life! I looked at him with new interest. Why, when men go in for that sort of thing, do they so generally pick stenographers or clerks? It has always seemed a little too convenient to me, but then most men are lazy about one thing or another.

Herbert's face became dyed with a dull rich crimson as he sat there in his high-backed chair at the head of the table.

"My friendship with Miss Sutton can be of no interest to the people assembled here unless it is the morbidly curious," Herbert ended with a look in my direction. He had carried it off with more dignity and poise than I believed he could manage.

"That's where you are wrong, Mr. Hastings. It is of vital interest to me and the people connected with the store. Do you know why she was so friendly with Carl Briggs?"

Herbert winced at that.

"No," he answered.

"Did she tell you anything to-day which might have some bearing on this case?"

"No."

"Did you see her this morning just before you went into Mrs. Briggs' office?"

"No."

"She was out there in the receiving-room talking to Briggs. You were in Mrs. Briggs' office this morning, weren't you?" Peter's question was definite.

"Yes." Herbert's face had been drained of all color as the questions and their implications were piled at him.

"What were you doing there?"

"I was trying to prevent a scandal," Herbert replied.

"A personal one?" Peter asked.

Herbert didn't answer. Peter's voice was relentless as he went on. "We have already discussed this, you and I, but when we had our last talk I didn't know some of the things which have since come to light.. If you had nothing to hide, why didn't you tell me about your visit to Mrs. Briggs just before the store opened?"

"I didn't want to become involved in her death, since I had nothing to do with it," Herbert answered, making a very neat point, too.

"You are involved, Mr. Hastings, greatly involved. You were having an argument with Mrs. Briggs this morning. You were overheard by Mr. Charles Doane. He left the suite of offices and paused on the balcony You looked up and saw him. You were suddenly afraid. You hurried up here, took one of the poison darts from the plaque in his office and fixed it in the pad on his chair."

Herbert's eyes were swelling. I'd never seen eyes pop before. I was afraid they would burst as I watched them with fascination.

"You were in that private office at the head of the balcony watching for the arrival of young Briggs. You knew about the acoustic peculiarities of that small window. When you were certain that Briggs was about to say something which would have incriminated you, you shot him and dropped the gun down the shaft."

There were loop-holes in Peter's story. They flashed through my mind as I watched the faces of the others listening so intently to Peter's accusation of Herbert.

Banter's mouth was open. The man probably has adenoids. Kramer's expression was one of amazed incredulity. John Grover was smirking. I think he enjoyed Herbert's discomfiture. Sandy McCleod looked like a small boy who has just been told that there is no Santa Claus. Herbert was completely overwhelmed.

"Before you killed Briggs, however, you had a busy morning," Peter went on. "There was one other person who could incriminate you and that was Willie Evans. You knew his habits. You followed him to the basement where he eats his lunch and killed him and then threw his body down the chute to fall into the baler. Your plans for the death of Mr. Doane had miscarried. You were worried. What have you done with him? Where is he?"

"You don't believe all this!" Herbert finally managed to gasp. "You know I did none of these things."

"I'm not joking, Mr. Hastings. Where is Charles Doane?"

A door at the side of the room opened and in popped Charlie Doane with a tray containing bottles of Scotch, Rye, charged water and ice. Behind him I could see Beth in a small kitchenette with a second tray containing glasses.

"Did I hear my name?" he asked.

I could have curled the smug young devil.

"Thank God, you're alive!" Herbert sighed with heartfelt relief. For a moment I thought he was going to faint.

"There goes your case," Grover said to Peter, whose face was an interesting study.

"Or just beginning," Peter answered. He turned to Charlie, "This is hardly a time for pranks, Mr. Doane."

"Pranks?" Charlie asked with a fine display of innocence.

"We thought you were dead, both of you," I answered his question.

"I was fixing that drink I promised you," he beamed at me, "and being careful at the same time."

"Then give it to me and let's get on with our meeting," I said testily; "that is, if Mr. Conklin is through."

"I'm finished for the moment," Peter answered.

"How about a drink?" Charlie asked Peter.

"Scotch and soda," he answered.

I was busy looking at the men and their clothes. Banter, Herbert and Charlie were wearing varying shades of gray. Grover's suit was beige tan. Kramer's a dark brown, Sandy's a pepper-and-salt mixture which might be called gray. If Mrs. Doyle's memory was correct our suspects were narrowed down to three men. Banter, Herbert and Charlie. Which one would she recognize?

Grover took a cigarette from a package on the table and reached into his pocket for a match. You've seen men slap their pockets when they can't find a thing they are sure should be part of their Tom Sawyer pocket collection. Grover was like that.

Charlie handed me some Rye with very little water and said, "We can begin any time."

Kramer and Sandy went toward the door. Banter followed them.

"This is no time to hold a meeting," Grover grumbled. "How can we concentrate on anything, under the circumstances?"

"A drink will calm you," Charlie said. "What will it be?"

"Scotch," he answered.

"You're staying to the meeting," Charlie said to Peter. "I have some data which I think will interest you."

The telephone rang. It wasn't in the cards for us to have that meeting. Herbert answered the telephone, hung up the receiver and said, "There's a Mrs. Doyle outside who is complaining that she can't stay here all night." He looked toward me.

I'd forgotten all about her and jumped to my feet. With a look at Peter which I knew he'd understand I said, "I think Grover is right. We ought to give up the idea of the meeting for to-night, at least."

Peter nodded. "Finish your drinks," I said as I took a last regretful sip of mine and put it down.

Peter held the door open for me, "Don't let her get away again," he warned.

They say women and elephants never forget, but I think some men have very long memories.

I expected to find Mrs. Doyle indignantly watching the gate at the entrance to the offices, but she was not there. She was down the aisle inspecting the price tags on mirrors, console tables, chests and other odd bits of furniture which lined the partition. I hurried toward her because I wanted her to be sitting down ready to watch the men as they came out.

There is nothing quite as deserted as a department store after closing hours unless it is a seaside resort on a rainy day. The floor was empty except for the rather lumbering figure of Mrs. Doyle. The hum and racket which had been the very pulse of the store all day long had ceased and it seemed strangely quiet to me as I went through the little gate toward Mrs. Doyle.

Mrs. Doyle was busy moving along a line of Hope Chests, I believe they are called. Rather atrocious things made of cedar. She lifted the lid of one, jumped back as if she had been struck and emitted a noise halfway between a yell and a groan. The lid banged down and Mrs. Doyle started in my direction, a look of fear on her face. She wore great flat shoes and in addition to her bunions I'm sure she had fallen arches. At any rate, her toe caught in the runner and she pitched forward, crashed into me, and down we both went in the aisle. The impact of her body knocked the wind out of me. My stomach ached frightfully for a moment. I heard a hollow crack and then knew nothing more until I was being revived in the store infirmary.

The first thing I remember was the smelling-salts being held under my nose by Beth Oliver. I pushed her hand away and tried to sit up.

"Better be quiet," she warned.

"What happened?" I asked.

I raised myself on one elbow. Across the little room on a second bed I saw the rounded bulk of Mrs. Doyle. A doctor was working over her. He had a stethoscope in his ears and was listening to her heart.

Peter and Charlie were watching anxiously.

I was dizzy for a moment and then sat up.

"What happened?" Peter asked, turning to me.

"I don't know." I explained as best I could, what I had seen and what had happened.

Peter, after hearing me out, went over to the doctor and asked about Mrs. Doyle.

"Her heart's bad," he said. "It won't be safe to talk to her for at least a half-hour after she comes to. She'll be out of it now in a few minutes. I've given her a stimulant."

I could hear Mrs. Doyle mumbling.

"I'll have a look at those chests," Peter said.

The door had just closed behind him when the lights went out all over the floor.

I heard some one say, "Damnation!" and I'm sure it was Peter. I heard other voices asking about the light switch and all that. I have never before been engulfed in such complete darkness. It was a solid black curtain. There was a general scurrying outside and then Mrs. Doyle began.

"Where am I?" she asked.

"You've had an accident," the doctor replied.

"Is it me eyes?" she asked.

"No."

"I can't see a thing. I'm blind as a bat." She seemed to be bordering on hysteria.

"Your eyes are quite all right," the doctor assured her. "Something happened to the lights. They'll be turned on again in a minute. Please be quiet."

I expected Mrs. Doyle to make further arguments, but she didn't. She remained quiet while I wondered why the lights were so long in coming on.

The store infirmary is on the sixth floor, across the building from the executive offices. I could hear voices vaguely and a faint sound of movement, but nothing definite. I slid my feet over the edge of the cot and bumped them into some one. It was Beth.

"Better be quiet," she advised.

"Heaven knows what I'm missing!" I replied. "Let's go out there. These lights ought to come on any minute."

They didn't, however. I don't know exactly how long they were off, but it seemed like five minutes or longer to me.

While we waited Beth told me what had happened while I was unconscious after being knocked down by Mrs. Doyle.

When Beth had finished I called in a stage-whisper, "Doctor, may I speak to Mrs. Doyle?"

"Shhh," he cautioned. "She's dozing again."

There in that Stygian darkness with nothing to divert my attention I had a chance to do some thinking. I tried to find the answers to a number of questions. What had terrified Mrs. Doyle? There was some one person on the sixth floor who knew the answer. Was that why the lights had gone out? Of course it was. Then who had been away from the group long enough to throw a switch or whatever it was that had happened?

When the lights finally came on I slid from the cot. Beth and I went outside immediately.

Across the building I could see dim forms moving. They were in the aisle near the executive offices. Beth and I went over. Charlie was nursing a slightly swollen jaw, rubbing it ruefully as a man will who has been unexpectedly hurt.

"I had a mix-up," he said with a grin.

When the lights went off so suddenly Charlie felt certain the sudden darkness had something to do with the chests in the aisle. With that idea in his mind he started off across the floor. Peter and Smith, bent on the same mission, were on their way when the lights went out. Charlie, knowing the building, had cut across the floor while Peter and Smith used the aisles, feeling, groping their way. Although they were the first to start, Charlie arrived on the spot before they reached it. He stopped and listened. The place was still pitch-black and he hoped to detect the sound of cautious movement. He heard the sound of footsteps moving carefully and almost soundlessly. Charlie waited tensed for action. Suddenly he heard a man breathing. Charlie reached out and grabbed the man. They struggled for several minutes, his opponent getting one good one to Charlie's jaw. Charlie finally downed him and was sitting on his chest when the glow from Peter's flashlight revealed his identity. It was Smith. A short time after that the lights were turned on again.

After the scuffle Charlie, Smith and Peter looked in every chest on that aisle and found nothing. Naturally they were baffled, wondering what it was that Mrs. Doyle had seen to upset her so. It could have been a mouse, of course, and I suggested that. Peter sneered openly.

"Stronger and hardier women than Mrs. Doyle have been frightened by mice," I reminded him. "And don't forget," I added, "elephants don't like mice."

"We'll soon find out what it was," Peter said with determination and headed for the infirmary.

As we followed him, there was something about the way Beth looked at Charlie's jaw which gave me an idea of the way the wind was blowing in that quarter.

# CHAPTER FIFTEEN

When we had all gathered in a half-circle outside the infirmary door, Peter stopped us. Just as he was about to speak the doctor came out and cautioned us to be silent because Mrs. Doyle still dozed. The doctor went back into the infirmary. The electrician with the fascinating overalls, gadgets and all, whom I had seen earlier in the day, came down the aisle.

"What happened to the lights?" Peter asked.

"Some one threw the main switch and pulled out several of the fuses for good luck," he explained.

"Where's the switch-box?"

"Over next to the elevators," the man answered.

It was a very bald statement, but it covered the situation completely.

"Smith," Peter called.

Smith bobbed into view from behind Herbert.

"Call Davis and have him come up here," he instructed. Then he turned to us. "I want to know where you were, all of you, just before and during the time the lights were out."

I was curious to see what the outcome of his questioning would be. He began with Herbert. "Where were you?" he asked.

"I went back to my office," Herbert replied.

"Weren't you concerned about this lady?" Peter pointed to me.

"Naturally, but she was in competent hands," Herbert answered.

"What did you do in your office?"

"I wanted to get something," Herbert answered.

"What?" Peter demanded impatiently.

"This." Herbert pulled a gun out of his pocket and held it before him rather threateningly, I thought.

"Do you have a permit?" Peter asked.

Herbert nodded.

"And what do you expect to do with the gun?" Peter went on.

"Protect myself," Herbert replied grimly.

"From what?" Peter demanded.

"That I can't answer."

For a moment I'll admit I suspected Herbert of wanting to commit suicide, but I was wrong. He loved life too dearly.

"How long were you in your office?" Peter continued.

"I don't know exactly. I was coming across the floor when the lights went out. I worked my way over here and waited."

"Did you see or were you seen by any one?" Peter asked.

Herbert looked at all of us as if he hoped to find corroboration somewhere. When no one spoke, after a brief wait, Peter grunted and turned to Grover.

"Where were you?" he asked.

"Over there sitting in an armchair," Grover replied.

Peter went on with his questions, but was unsuccessful in getting any important information. Banter went down to the fifth floor and didn't know that the lights were out. Kramer said he had been in the anteroom of the infirmary from the time we had been carried there until the lights went out. Sandy said he had hung around outside waiting for something to happen. It was Sandy who telephoned to the basement for the electrician. Beth and Charlie had carried me to the infirmary and were with me until the place was plunged into darkness.

If Peter was disappointed by the lack of information he was able to gather, he didn't show it. We were all of us waiting for his next move when the doctor came out to say that Mrs. Doyle was awake and could talk for a short time. He warned Peter not to excite her. As Peter turned toward the door, I stood up expectantly. He hesitated a moment before he nodded for me to follow him. Mrs. Doyle, more than a little confused, was sitting up in bed, her back bolstered by several pillows.

"Who knocked me down?" she demanded when she saw me.

"You tripped and knocked me down," I explained with a smile. "You fell."

"Did I now? Did I hurt you?" she asked solicitously.

"Knocked the wind out of me," I explained. "How's your head?"

"The head's all right. He says it's me heart. He won't let me get up." She gave the doctor a belligerent look.

"Do you feel able to talk?" Peter asked.

"And what is it I'm doing?" she countered.

"Then tell us what you saw out there. Miss Thomas says that something had upset you. You were hurrying toward her when you tripped and fell. What did you see?"

"The body of a girl stuffed into one of them boxes."

"Are you sure, Mrs. Doyle?" Peter seemed reluctant to believe her, and no wonder.

"Don't you think I know a body when I see one?" she flared. "She was all bent up, and since it's no place to take a nap, the girl must have been dead."

Peter and I exchanged a quick glance. The same thought was in both our minds.

"We've looked in those boxes, Mrs. Doyle. They're empty, all of them," Peter said quietly.

"I don't care what they are now. There was a girl in one of them," she insisted. "The first thing I know you'll be telling me I'm not here at all. I ought to have stayed home and minded me own business, anyhow, and I will the next time," she said emphatically.

She made a move to get out of the bed.

"Better continue to rest," the doctor warned.

"I've got some work to do," Peter said, and left the office.

I knew where he was going and I wanted to be with him. He was going to start a search for Eva Sutton's body.

"I wouldn't have come at all if it hadn't been for you," Mrs. Doyle said to me.

"I appreciate your coming," I assured her, but my mind was on Peter and what he would find out there. There was no telling where the body was by this time.

"After that man was shot this morning," she talked on, "I wanted no part of it at all. I left the store then and went home. I was telling my daughter, she's the one that lives home with me, what happened over a cup of tea when you arrived. I should have stayed home minding me own business." Her voice drowsed for a moment. "I'm that sleepy I can hardly keep me eyes open." She yawned sleepily.

"Why don't you rest a minute?" I suggested, for I was anxious to be with Peter.

"Maybe I will."

I pulled the pillows out from behind her back and in a minute she was sleeping. The doctor said it was the medicine he had given her.

Peter had started a search for the missing body. Everybody was busy when I went out onto the floor. I saw Peter in the aisle where Mrs. Doyle and I had fallen and went directly to him.

He had been making a careful search of all the chests and looked up from one as I approached him. "Do you remember which one she was looking at as you approached her?" he asked.

I showed him the chest.

"I thought so," he said.

He went to another chest. I followed. "Bend over close to me when I open the next one," he said in a lowered voice.

I did as I was told. He lifted the lid and I leaned forward. "I found some hair in the chest you indicated. I want you to do a job for me. Go to every man who was with us in that office this afternoon and look for hair on his clothes. Your eyes all right?" he asked.

I had to laugh at him; I couldn't help it. He was so

anxious. I assured him I'd always been able to see more than I should most of the time, and went off on my errand.

Herbert was across an aisle and I went to him as he moved along peering onto and under day beds, sofas and couches.

"Why did you get the gun?" I asked.

He stopped and looked at me, defiantly I thought.

"I learned a lot when Conklin was accusing me of having killed Charlie. The same powers would like to get rid of me, too," he said.

"What powers?" I asked quickly, hoping he would have something to tell me.

"You don't suppose I'd be wasting my time if I were sure, do you?" he asked logically enough.

"You must have some idea," I insisted.

"Do you suspect me?" he asked.

I did and I didn't and my answer was truthful enough. I told him I had no idea why so many people had been killed.

He came very close to me and said, "You've never liked me very much; I suppose you'll think less of me now."

"Because of the girl?" I asked.

He nodded.

I put my hand on his shoulder as my eyes looked for a tell-tale hair somewhere on his coat front. As my eyes searched my tongue was saying, "I've lived too long to pass judgment on any one, Herbert. What you do or have done is your business and none of mine, but if you must have a mistress again, I'd advise you to get one away from the store." I brushed his shoulder with the tips of my fingers as I released my hand. I'm sure it was a natural gesture which did not betray my questing eyes.

"I have a theory of my own," he said.

"Why don't you tell Peter?" I asked.

"Because he suspects me," he replied.

"He suspects all of us. He was quite sure all day that

Charlie was the murderer and would have gone on thinking so if Charlie hadn't hidden to protect himself," I explained.

"So he shifts his suspicions to me. I can't prove my innocence," he mused. "But I've got an idea."

"It may be very important. See Peter and tell him," I advised. "Poor lad, he's about at the end of his rope. A little help won't make him mad. Do it now," I urged. As he turned away I clutched at a hair on his sleeve just above the crook of his elbow. It was at the place where a person's head would lie if carried in a man's arms.

When I had the hair I didn't know what to do with it. You can't put one down and expect to find it when you come back. I hunted everywhere for a place and my anxious eye spotted a telephone directory. The prize I had clutched from Herbert's arm was put on the page at the beginning of the H's.

I've played treasure hunt in my time and all sorts of games about clues, but never had I taken them as seriously as I did that early evening as I roamed about the sixth floor of Doane's seeking first one man and then another, looking for hairs. My success with Herbert increased my zeal as I sought out Kramer and talked to him. The man must have been a distant relative of Bluebeard himself, because I found all sorts and varieties of hairs plastered all over him. The man couldn't have been very familiar with a clothes-brush, as I'm sure the crop I reaped was not a one-day collection.

I filed my find under the K's and went looking for John Grover, who was very businesslike in his method of searching. He wasn't very cordial. In fact, he seemed to resent my presence and finally asked me if I was checking up on him. His collar bulged a little at the back of his neck. On the inside of the bulge I could see a white thread. I'd have probably pulled it out for any other man, but not Grover. I asked him what, in his opinion, was the reason for the tremendous slump in Doane's profits.

"Bad business," he answered.

"Charlie doesn't think so," I said.

He turned and faced me more annoyed than ever, and said, "What does he know about it? He just came home, didn't he?"

He didn't stay still very long at a time, but I managed as best I could. I kept him talking and heard things that meant very little to me, but were, I suppose, important to any one interested in department stores. Among the things he mentioned were unit sales, dollar volume, mark up, etc.

When I finally left him I had one hair to carry off with me to file in the telephone directory under G.

They were nearing the end of the hunt when I approached Banter. There was a nice hair curled on his shoulder just at the edge of his collar. My problem was to get it without arousing his suspicion. I'd been so successful with the others that I began to doubt my luck.

"It's a bit like hunting for a needle in a haystack, isn't it?" I asked.

"It's sheer foolishness," he replied. "If there was a body here whoever tried to hide it was a fool."

He had just closed the lower part of a corner cupboard and stood up.

"I feel a bit faint," I murmured and leaned toward him, my hand out.

"Steady," he warned. "Why don't you sit down?"

"I'll be all right in a minute. Just let me hold on to you."

He leaned forward and was nicely solicitous. That gave me my chance to get the hair.

"You've been doing too much for one day," he said. "After all, you're no flapper."

I said something about being as young as you feel and left him. I had a sample from each of them and hoped they would be helpful to Peter. I picked up my telephone book and went looking for him. He met me in the main aisle.

"Get anything?" he asked.

"In here, filed alphabetically." I thrust the book toward him.

"Good. I've another job for you."

He led me to a chair, which I'll admit I was grateful to use. He stood in front of me. "You keep your eyes peeled in back of me. I'll be able to see in back of you. You haven't tunnel vision, have you?" he asked.

"I don't know what it is, but if you mean not being able to see to the right or left, no," I replied.

"Don't let any one get close to us without warning me," he cautioned.

# CHAPTER SIXTEEN

Peter's eyes were looking over and beyond me. I was dying with curiosity. What more could I do for him? What was his plan?

He bent a little closer and asked, "Is the coast all clear?"

I nodded and whispered, "Haven't you found the body?"

"No," he replied, "but I'll come to that later. This is more important. I've been talking to the doctor about Mrs. Doyle. He says it would be a grave mistake to move her to-night. She's had a bad shock and should be kept quiet. I suggested keeping her here, to which he has agreed. I've sent for her daughter and that's where you come in."

I didn't see what I could do, under the circumstances, and started to tell him so. "But—" I began, when he stopped me.

"Just be patient." He made me feel about six. I gave him an all-right-teacher look and waited. "Mrs. Doyle may be able to help us with the first murder. I don't know, but she's more important now than she was before. As you know, we've been shy of clues. As I see it now, the field has narrowed down to elimination and proof. These hairs will be a help, but they'll be thin evidence at best."

"Are you punning?" I asked. He was so serious that he had to stop for a minute and consider what I meant. He gave me a sickish grin which showed his annoyance and went on.

"Our murderer has been covering himself all day and he's been doing an excellent job of it. I don't want him to suspect what we know, which is little enough, God knows."

I gave him a look of agreement.

"I'd like you to stay here to-night with Mrs. Doyle if you think you'll be able to stand it."

I was puzzled. If he had sent for the woman's daughter, why did he want me? "I can stand it, all right, but why?" I asked, nettled by his doubts of my powers of endurance.

He grinned at me and was more like himself than he had been for hours. "I think the murderer will want to move the body again."

"Good Lord!" I exclaimed. "Why?"

"Why did he take it out of the chest where Mrs. Doyle saw it?" he asked.

Of course I had no answer to that.

"He'll come back for the body, all right," Peter assured me. "And that's where you come in. I'm glad we didn't find it. I'm sure it's hidden on this floor somewhere."

"Just where do I come in?" I asked, not being able to see his line of reasoning.

"It will be natural for you to stay with Mrs. Doyle. She's your witness, you've been mixed up in this thing all day. I want extra people watching for me. I don't want to post policemen all over this floor, for if I do the murderer will take to cover. I'll pretend that we must stay here because of Mrs. Doyle. I'll keep Davis and Smith with me. If you'll stay and keep your eyes open, that will make four of us."

"Can I tell Charlie?" I asked.

"I'd rather you didn't."

I agreed to that, but I thought he was wrong and told him so. "If the murderer has an ounce of sense," I said, "he'll leave well enough alone."

"He hasn't sense in the way you mean," Peter said. "This man's idea is to cover up. The entire day has been planned on that basis. It began with the death of Mrs. Briggs. She was killed to cover something. The death of the son was for the same reason. Willie was killed because he was in a position to expose the murderer. This girl was killed because she knew too much. She was one of the last people in the office with Mrs. Briggs if we can believe her. Don't you see what he has been doing? He's been carefully covering his trail all day. He not only killed Willie, but he tried to do away with the body. I don't know the terms psychologists use to describe him. I haven't studied as much as I wish I had, but I do know this: the man's mind is working on a single track. He's hipped on the subject of covering up something he's done. If things hadn't happened so fast and so furiously to-day we might have been able to get to his motive. We are pretty sure now that it has to do with the store. The murderer is going to be uneasy until he disposes of the body in such a way that it can't possibly seem to be connected with him. Imagine how you would feel if you had transferred it from one hiding-place to another and expected any moment to have some one find it?"

"I wouldn't have done it that way," I said.

I've often put myself in the position of a murderer and thought about what I would have done under the circumstances. A case of hindsight again.

"I'd stake my life that the man is waiting to get the body out of here. I'm sure of it—so sure that I'm willing to gamble my success on the idea. If we're smart we can catch our man red-handed," he finished, hypnotized by his idea.

I was still skeptical. "Wait a minute," I stopped him. "Did you notice the clothes the men were wearing?" He nodded. "Banter, Herbert and Charlie are wearing gray suits,"

"McLeod's might look gray in some lights," he interrupted.

I was willing to admit the truth of that, but there was something else on my mind. "Why," I asked, "did the murderer permit Eva Sutton to live all day?"

"Perhaps he didn't know she had seen him," Peter suggested.

"Either that or—" I began, when a horrible realization seized me. I remembered that whispering window. While

he had talked about Mrs. Doyle, the gray suit, Eva Sutton
and Carl Briggs in the office I had thought the window
was open. Later when I looked up at it again it was
closed.

"Stay with me," Peter chided. "If your thoughts are
worth anything let me in on them."

"Peter," I started. I had to talk about it. I told him
about that little window and my fears. "If Eva Sutton is
the girl Mrs. Doyle saw in that chest, then I—"

"Don't be hysterical," he said scathingly. It was nice of
him. He was doing it to put me at ease.

"But, Peter, we didn't come up immediately. The
murderer had plenty of time to come up here, kill her,
and stuff her into one of those chests."

Peter assured me that the girl was probably killed
before we had our conversation downstairs after my
return from getting Mrs. Doyle. I hope Peter is right. It
would be too horrible to think that I was responsible for
the death of that poor creature. My mind ran to her,
anyhow.

She had seemed so worn and undernourished-looking
when I had first seen her. I became indignant with
Herbert. The least he could have done was to feed her
properly. Poor child. Had her fear and her terror been
connected with Herbert all the time?

Peter interrupted my thinking. "If Hastings didn't kill
all these people, and for the moment I'm willing to give
him the benefit of the doubt, who else would want to kill
on a wholesale scale?"

"I don't know," I answered wearily. "My head is too
full of too many things."

"Maybe you shouldn't stay here, after all." He was
nicely considerate if a bit calculating as he said it.

"I'll stay. I'll be all right, but how about some dinner?
I need food."

"Get your precious Charlie to take you out," he
suggested. "You can come back later, ostensibly to be with
Mrs. Doyle. I may not be able to talk to you again to-

night, so let's get it fixed now. I'll pick a spot for you and suggest that you take a rest. When I do that it will be your turn to watch. I'll have a flashlight for you to carry in your bag. If you hear anything odd use the flash but keep yourself covered. I don't want you shot," he warned.

"This floor is so large that a dozen men could move about on it and I'd neither see nor hear them," I objected.

"We'll take care of that," he assured me. "No one will move about on this floor without making some noise, rest assured of that. If and when you hear a noise, crouch down behind your resting-place and turn on your flash. Protect yourself," he warned again.

The promise of danger and excitement thrilled me. "I'll do it," I promised. "I'll go to dinner now. I need a pick-me-up. I only had half of that drink Charlie gave me."

"Okay. How long will you be?"

"An hour or two," I answered.

"Bring Doane back with you. He's not out of the woods yet. Remember, he's wearing a gray suit." He grinned as he said it, but his grin was only half fun.

I didn't answer him.

"Don't be too long," he said as I stood up.

I was tired and didn't propose going to some cheap place where we could eat quickly. I wanted the luxury of fine linen, good silver and crystal. I felt tired and dirty. I'd been roaming about a dust-laden department store all day, and while I wouldn't have missed any of it for the world, at the same time I wasn't going to rush right back for the night's vigil, body or no body, and furthermore it seemed to me to be something which would be done in the small hours of the night.

With the telephone book under his arm Peter moved along beside me toward the infirmary. We had the entire floor to ourselves, which made me feel safe to ask, "Aren't you staking rather a lot on to-night?"

"It's going to simplify things a good deal if I can catch the murderer red-handed," he replied.

"And you think it's Herbert Hastings?" I ventured

suggestively.

"Your guess is as good as mine," he replied.

We said no more because we were nearing the others.

Charlie was talking to Beth when we approached. The others were standing about as if they expected something to happen. Smith and Sandy were together. They seemed to hit it off very well. Davis was sprawled out on a divan and I think he was asleep. I don't know that they ever did, but certainly after that night's business Doane's should have had a second-hand furniture sale. Everything near the infirmary was well used.

"Any luck?" Peter asked Smith.

Davis' eyes blinked open, but he didn't get up. Poor chap, I suppose he believed in snatching his sleep when he could get it. He didn't know it then, but he was in for an all-night session.

"Did any of you find anything?" Peter asked the group.

They just sort of wagged their heads disconsolately.

"Bodies don't fly away," Peter said and there was disgust and annoyance in his voice. He was a good actor, that lad.

"Can you be sure there was a body?" Charlie asked.

"She said she saw one," Peter snapped.

"The doctor says she's very ill," Herbert cut in. "Perhaps she imagined it."

"Then why were the lights tampered with?" Peter flashed back. "Some one threw the switch and then pulled out the fuses so we couldn't have any light. For all we know, the body may be in the Hudson River by now."

"That's a bit far-fetched," Charlie said and it sounded annoying. If he had tried he couldn't have played into Peter's hand any better than he did.

"It may sound far-fetched to you, Mr. Doane, but I believe anything can happen in this store. If the body is in the store, it will be found." He turned to Smith. "Get extra men and have them posted at every door that leads to the street." He turned back to Charlie and asked a horrible question. "Is there an incinerator in the building?"

I've a good strong constitution and can stand most anything, but that question sent cold shivers up and down my spine. I asked Peter about it later and he said it just occurred to him at the moment. You see, he was anxious for the murderer to show his hand and hoped that the mention of the incinerator might give the murderer an idea if he hadn't already thought of it. I'm old-fashioned, I know, in many ways. I've lived a long time and I have seen many things developed. When I hear about the air-cooled trains that whisk you across the sun-baked deserts now and think back to the hot horrible boxes in which I first crossed the country I wonder if I'm living in the same world. There are so many things I accept to-day which I was skeptical about yesterday.

I saw the automobile and airplane develop from nothing. Tunnels have gone under rivers and dirigibles have crossed the ocean. Men play hermit at the North or South Pole and we are in touch with them by radio. Such things are every-day occurrences. So many things are common to us all now and accepted, but there is one thing I will not accept and that is the modern idea of cremation. I know it's supposed to be sanitary and has been in vogue for centuries in one form or another, but the family plot in Woodlawn is good enough for me. Some one of my ancestors bought a great big plot. He must have been ambitious at the time or else graves were cheaper than they are now. At any rate, that's where I'm going. The idea of that girl and the incinerator turned my blood cold.

Charlie didn't answer Peter's question. He obviously didn't know. John Grover said there was one.

"Isn't Mrs. Doyle any better?" I asked Peter.

"No. She'll have to stay here all night. The doctor doesn't want her moved."

"But will she stay?" I asked, trying to be very innocent.

"She'll have to stay," Peter said grimly.

"Then I'll stay with her," I announced.

"There's no need of that," Peter said.

"Nevertheless I'm staying," I said with determination.

"But, Ethel—" Charlie began to remonstrate.

"Don't argue with me, young man. You can take Miss Oliver and me to dinner and bring me back here later."

"What's she got to do with it, anyhow?" Herbert asked.

I was suddenly afraid for Mrs. Doyle. That phase had never occurred to me before. Poor woman! She was in danger. Had Peter thought of that? There was only one person who could know why she was in the store. The murderer. If he had been listening at that little window, he knew Mrs. Doyle had seen him. It was an awful responsibility. Something had to be done to protect the woman.

"It was just a foolish idea of mine," I said quickly. "After young Briggs was shot I looked up and saw her on the balcony. I told Mr. Conklin about her and he had her brought here."

"Wasn't she the woman you brought—?" Smith started to ask and stopped in the middle of his speech. He was standing next to Davis and that sleepy young man had kicked him a good vicious flip on the shin.

Drat the man, anyhow! He had probably spoiled my lying.

I took hold of Peter's arm and said, "Tell your man to let me in when I come back." I dragged him along the aisle with me. Over my shoulder I called to Charlie and said, "Come, Charlie, and bring Miss Oliver with you."

As they started to follow us I whispered to Peter, "That woman is in danger. Keep her guarded every minute. Her life isn't worth two cents. Remember the little window."

"You're great," he whispered and gave my arm a squeeze. I bruise easily and he hurt, but I didn't mind. It was a heartfelt compliment to an old woman who had probably been a nuisance all day.

# CHAPTER SEVENTEEN

We went to the St. Regis, where I could get what I wanted. Charlie suggested that new place in Rockefeller Center overlooking the fountain, but I just couldn't bear the thought of that.

We settled down and I had two side-cars. A silly name for a drink, but they do work fast. Perhaps some wag did name them after those bathtub contraptions I occasionally see people riding in. I should think a motorcycle was bad enough, but one of those things—ugh! It makes me ill to think of them.

We had a good dinner. Charlie attended to that. We were all hungry and had very little to say until we trifled over our dessert. I had had all I wanted of mine and sat back and demanded,

"Why did you hide this afternoon?"

"I wondered when you would ask that question." He grinned at me, with the crinkling of his eyes which I adore. I tell you right now if I were younger that grin of Charlie's would make me act like a fool.

"Out with it." I rummaged in my bag for cigarettes. I like to smoke, but never during a meal, because I hate to spoil the flavor of good food with tobacco fumes.

"It was really my fault," Beth spoke up.

"So the woman tempted you," I accused Charlie.

"I'd hardly call it that," he answered.

"I told Mr. Doane the things this afternoon that I promised to tell you to-morrow night," Beth said.

"I thought I had missed something," I said, and they both laughed. I looked at my watch. "Tell me," I commanded. "We haven't much time."

"Briefly it's this," Charlie began, and then turned to Beth and said with that sweet considerate way he has, "If I miss anything be sure to check up on me."

I could tell that they had progressed a long way along the road called romance since early in the afternoon. I was a little jealous, I'll admit. Up to that time except for a probable fly-by-night I'd been the only woman in Charlie's life.

"Miss Oliver," Charlie started his story, "has been sure for a long time that there was something rotten in the state of Doane. There were shortages and thefts in the jewelry department. Mrs. Briggs had been suspicious of several clerks, but was never able to prove anything. When she complained about the clerks to the personnel office they were transferred, not fired. Mrs. Briggs had talked to other buyers about general conditions in the store and they all agreed that something was going on that was not regular, but what, they did not know.

"Mrs. Briggs even discussed the matter with Herbert, but he insisted that she was imagining things. He said that business was bad, and could not or would not believe that there was a general store-wide thieving campaign going on. Mrs. Briggs told Miss Oliver that there were heavy inventory losses in the men's furnishings, handkerchief, drugs and perfumes and many other departments throughout the store where small expensive merchandise was carried."

"What's your idea?" I asked Charlie.

"It seems like a racket to me," he answered.

"Racket?" I asked, not seeing just how a racket would work in that way. My idea of a racket was gangsters shooting people in Times Square or in the Loop District of Chicago.

"There are all sorts of rackets," he said. "I don't know that Doane's has been the victim of one, but it seems quite likely. This particular racket, I believe, was to let the store run down so that control could be bought very cheaply."

"Herbert?" I asked.

"It seems probable, although I hate to believe it. He must have known what was going on and yet did nothing to stop it," he answered reluctantly.

"How much of the conversation did you overhear from the board-room this afternoon, before you popped in on us?" I asked.

"You mean about Herbert and Miss Sutton?" I nodded.

"Plenty, but I don't see what that would have to do with it," he replied.

"If you don't, I do. Get the check. I want to get back to the store," I said.

"Why the rush?"

"Herbert Hastings may be a fool. I've always thought so, but he's not as big a fool as you seem to think. If he was mixed up with that Sutton girl, it is reason enough for anything that has happened to-day."

"Then you suspect Herbert."

"If Herbert is the murderer he has more gumption than I credit him with. On the other hand it is quite likely that he has been a tool in the hands of some smart crook. Don't you see the Sutton girl was probably the club which has been held over his head all along?"

"Just what are you driving at?"

"Pay the check. I'll tell you as we drive back to the store." I stood up and a waiter came toward us slowly, never once forgetting the dignity which should be his within the sacred portals of that old hotel.

On the way down the Avenue Charlie asked, "Are you thinking of Banter?"

"He's the personnel man, isn't he?" I replied. "He's the one man who could hire, fire and shift the help about in the store. What has he been doing all day? Why was that Sutton girl so afraid? We've been blind. We've had the reason right under our noses and have been too busy running from one murder to another to see it. I want to see Peter Conklin. Oh, how I wish we had had that store meeting this morning!" I didn't stop talking as we climbed into a cab.

"We wouldn't have had the information we have now,"

he reminded me. "We know what we know because of Miss Oliver."

"I'm not trying to slight Miss Oliver's importance to us. We'd have been put on the right track and could have unearthed the information." I turned to Beth then and asked, "Do you think Carl Briggs was an honest man?"

"I don't know."

"You were married to him, weren't you?"

"He wasn't honest with me."

I wanted to ask her why she had ever married him, but didn't. I went on with the business at hand.

"Don't you see it?" I asked them both. "Briggs was one of the men they used to carry merchandise out of the store. He was known. He could come in and out of the store any time he pleased. He knew the girls. He took them out. He talked to them. They passed stolen goods over to him and he got rid of it for them. Mrs. Briggs must have found it out in some way." I turned to Beth. "This theory will explain the package of jewels left at the hotel for you. Briggs wanted to be rid of them. Don't you think I'm right?"

Before she could answer, Charlie asked, "How did Mrs. Briggs discover the truth?"

"I don't know; only I'm sure I'm right. It all fits together. Carl Briggs probably hated everything connected with the name of Doane. When he threatened to sue the store or whatever it was he was going to do, they found a perfect tool for their plan."

"Who?" Charlie insisted.

I was annoyed with him. I was so excited. My mind was racing ahead trying to put the pieces together and he asked me stupid questions. "Banter, Herbert, any one," I snapped back at him and went on. "Briggs wasn't working and yet he had money, which made his mother suspicious." I turned to Beth. "These girls who were transferred from your department, were they friends of Briggs?"

"Some of them were," she admitted; "but I don't see

where Eva Sutton enters the picture."

"She was probably the liaison officer between a man higher up in the store and Briggs. If she was interested in Herbert, how else can we explain her connections with Carl Briggs? Do you think he was in love with her?" I asked.

"He wasn't in love with any one. I don't know anything about his relationship with Eva Sutton. It may have been purely business. They were friendly when I first knew him, but nothing more."

"These other girls," I asked with more brutality than was necessary, "were they platonic friendships, too?"

"I don't believe so. His interest in other women was one of my reasons for giving him a free hand."

"Did Mrs. Briggs ever visit your apartment?" I asked her.

"When we left the store last night she said she was going there," Beth replied. "But that was because I had left him. She was furious and wanted to see him."

"There we have it all." I was gleeful. "Mrs. Briggs called on her son unexpectedly last night. Without you there, he became careless. The Lord only knows what she found. It was enough. The jig was up. Briggs probably told his cronies by telephone. That's why the woman was murdered. Her death was made to look like suicide. If the truth had not been discovered about her death, Briggs would have been brought in and done away with or—" The cab pulled up at the employees' entrance to the store and I had to stop what Charlie called my romancing.

As Beth and I waited for him to pay the cab it occurred to me that he had not answered my question. He had told me his ideas about what was happening in the store, but he had said nothing about his reasons for hiding.

I stopped him there on the curb and repeated my question.

"Just a precaution," he said. "I felt certain that Willie would not be found. It was obvious that the murderer was covering his trail. The man must be mad. There is no other explanation for the things which have happened. A meeting and a survey of the books would start things. With me out of the way that meeting would not be called. I just decided to vanish for a few hours, and fearing that Miss Oliver and myself might have been overheard I took her with me. No one thought of looking in that kitchenette."

"Umm." I was thinking. I turned to him. "Take me up to the sixth floor and then go home, and for heaven's sake, take care of yourself."

"If you think I'm going home you're crazy. I wouldn't miss this night for anything." He steered us toward the door.

"What could happen?" I asked sharply.

"Anything. I won't leave you here alone."

"I won't be alone. Peter and the police will be here. I'm going to sit with a sick woman who has been dragged into this mess because of an idea of mine."

"And I'm going to watch a friend of mine who was dragged into the mess because she bought some of my stock. Come along." He took us each by an arm and piloted us through the door, where a glum-faced policeman was standing guard.

As we stepped out of the elevator on the sixth floor it presented a gloomy appearance. One light burned in front of the elevators. The rest of the floor was in darkness except for the lights in the infirmary and a few still burning in the executive offices.

I saw Peter sitting on the divan in the aisle just outside the infirmary. I wanted to talk to him. Leaving the others behind I barged on ahead. Mrs. Doyle's daughter, poised and dignified, was sitting there beside Peter.

"How is she?" I asked.

"Sleeping. The doctor says she's reacting beautifully," Peter answered.

"Is any one watching her?" I asked.

"The doctor is in there. She's all right."

"I want to talk to you, Peter. You'll excuse us?" I asked Miss Doyle.

We walked down the aisle and I told Peter the things I had heard from Charlie and my ideas about the motive for the crimes.

"You're probably right," he said thoughtfully, "but it makes it worse for your friend Herbert."

"Have you had any report on the hairs?" I asked anxiously.

"Not yet. We'll get them anytime now."

"Don't be too sure it's just Herbert," I warned.

"Meaning Banter, Grover and Kramer?" he asked.

"Any or all of them," I said.

"If Hastings would talk, it might help us," Peter said. "I tried to work on him while you were out, but he had nothing to say."

"If he is guilty he won't talk and if he knows anything he's probably scared for his life and doesn't dare tell what he knows."

"You're inclined to think he is the tool of the real murderer, aren't you?" Peter asked.

"Yes."

"That may be. We'll know before morning."

"But, Peter," I cautioned, "you don't want more murders, do you?"

"Good Lord, no! This has been a slaughter-house as it is."

"Then have Mrs. Doyle watched constantly, will you? She is in danger. Smith spoiled my effort to cover her. Herbert is either guilty himself or in danger. We can take no chances. I'm afraid."

"Want to quit?"

"Certainly not. I've never been known to quit," I boasted.

"Better get a little rest," he suggested. "I don't think things will happen until later in the night."

"Have they left?"

"Who?"

"Herbert, Kramer and Grover?"

"No; they're still here."

He led me back toward the divan. Charlie came up to me and said, "I'm going down and have a look at some records. I'll be back later."

I sat beside Miss Doyle and after some rambling hit-and-miss conversation we got down to cases and the thing which was on both our minds.

"Has your mother ever had one of these attacks before?" I asked.

"Two," the girl answered. "As you may have guessed, she is quite headstrong."

"I rather thought she had a mind of her own," I replied.

"Very definitely."

"I feel responsible for your mother," I told the girl. "I may have caused her all this trouble for nothing. Terrible things have happened, more may follow. I do hope she won't be seriously affected."

"She has strong recuperative powers," the girl assured me, and the next moment we had a definite demonstration of that fact, for over the partition came the determined voice of Mrs. Doyle.

"I won't stay here!" she declared lustily.

The girl and I went into the room at once.

"What are you doing here?" she demanded of her daughter.

"I came down to be with you," the girl replied.

"Well, you could have saved yourself, for I'm going home."

She kicked her feet out from under the coverlet and swung her legs over the side of the bed. I laughed; I couldn't help it. I hadn't seen a pair of old-fashioned drawers in years.

She sat back on the bed and pulled the sheet across her legs. "Where's my clothes?" she demanded.

"Over here," the doctor answered.

"Well, give them to me and get out," Mrs. Doyle ordered.

"Now, Mother," the girl protested.

"No sass now!" She stood up when the doctor had left. She sat down again quickly, a look of amazement on her red face.

"You mustn't exert yourself," I warned. "You've had a shock."

"I'm weak," she agreed, "and that's a fact. I don't know what's the matter with me."

"You must rest. You're going to stay here to-night. I'll take you home in the morning," the daughter promised. She reached into a bag, produced a long flannelette gown, in which Mrs. Doyle encased herself without protest.

The fight gone out of her, Mrs. Doyle lay back and permitted herself to be covered again.

"Did you give Denny his supper?" she asked after a minute.

"Yes."

Mrs. Doyle turned to me. "He's the youngest. Works nights he does."

She was quiet for a long time, her eyes closed. I thought she had gone to sleep and decided to leave her alone, forgetting for the moment my concern over her safety. I stood up and made motions of leaving to the daughter.

Mrs. Doyle opened her eyes and said, "Don't go."

After a few moments of quiet she turned to me and asked, "When am I going to look at the men? They may change their clothes to-morrow."

"The doctor will let us know. We don't want you to exert yourself for a little while." I was talking to fill in time.

"I think I'll know him." She was thoughtful for a minute or two and then said reminiscently. "I was fighting mad. If there's anything in the world I hate it's being bumped into with never a word of beggin' your pardon or the like. He was in a good bit of a hurry and went out by the door which I had entered. If I'd of had a brick I'd have fired it at him I was that mad. It was then I found the answer to me problem right there on the floor."

"What do you mean?" I asked eagerly.

"A nice bit of wire and just the right size for me leg," she replied. "There it is." She pointed to the chair which held her clothes.

I had a grim moment when I thought of Mrs. Briggs' throat and Mrs. Doyle's leg being of an approximate size.

"It's too bad you didn't get a good look at the man," I said.

"It's come to me now," she answered; "I'd know the back of him anywhere."

"Why?" I asked.

Before she could answer it happened. Something came hurtling over the top of the partition. I discovered later that it was one of those earthenware jars that sit in the bottom of a water-cooler to catch the excess water from the spigot.

Fortunately it missed all three of us as it struck the floor with a terrific crash.

# CHAPTER EIGHTEEN

Peter came rushing in to see what had happened. He took one look at the wreckage of the thing on the floor and demanded, "Where did that come from?"

I told him briefly. "I'll be right back." Peter dashed away. I called for the doctor, but he, good man, was right there. He had followed Peter into the room. The doctor went to Mrs. Doyle, who seemed all right except for some difficulty with her breathing. I could hear feet scurrying all over the sixth floor as men raced about trying to locate the person who had tried to kill one of us.

Peter came back and beckoned me to the door. "What happened?"

I told him about my conversation with Mrs. Doyle.

"Then the murderer knows why she's here. That crock was meant for her."

"Do be careful, won't you?" I begged. "I don't want that poor woman killed."

"She won't be killed if I can help it."

"We have the weapon," I said.

"What weapon?"

"The wire used to strangle Mrs. Briggs. It has been wrapped about Mrs. Doyle's leg all day holding up her stocking."

"Well, I'll be damned!" Peter exploded, and I knew exactly how he felt. He raced away once more.

The doctor was standing beside Mrs. Doyle. I knew I was not needed there. I had rather imagined we were safe in the infirmary, but since we were not, I decided to see why. If I had stopped to think I probably would not have been as brave as I was. Lack of thought and ignorance are often mistaken for courage. Probably Peter's hunt for the culprit outside made me forget that the man might very well be concealed somewhere in the infirmary. As I started my investigation I was interested in only one thing. How did the man get inside without some one seeing him?

The infirmary was walled off from the balance of the sixth floor by a ceiling-high partition. The hospital itself on the inside was partitioned to a height of probably eight feet. The person who had thrown that thing had been in the infirmary all the time or had entered it through some door we didn't know existed.

I went on a tour of inspection while the doctor and her daughter tried to soothe Mrs. Doyle. The room we had been in was on a corridor which led away from the reception room. I opened doors as I moved along. I was most interested in the room next to ours. It was a diet kitchen—at least, I believe that's what they are called. At any rate, there was a large electric icebox, an electric stove and in one corner a drinking fountain which held a five-gallon bottle of spring water. The drip stand was empty.

I was satisfied that that was the spot from which the missile had come. I went on down the little corridor opening doors and peering into vacant rooms. At the end of the rooms the passageway turned a corner and before me was a door. I opened it and found myself in the store opposite a staircase at the end of the elevators. I stepped out into the main part of the building and had a sinking feeling as I heard the door swing shut with a click of the latch.

I was locked out alone in a strange part of the building away from the others. If the murderer was lurking there my chances of ever getting back alive were very slim. I longed for a good old-fashioned hatpin. I have often bucked up my courage with the thought of what I could do defensively with one of them for a weapon.

For a moment I hoped that I was opposite the elevators which we had used when we came back from dinner. I wasn't. I was at the extreme end of the building away from the central side elevators and it seemed like a mile or more from the executive offices.

I moved along the partition, expecting a man to pop out at me with each step I took. It wasn't pitch-black because of the lights down in the central part of the building, but it was darker than I wanted it to be at the moment. I could hear voices far off and I did think of calling out, but decided against it. There was no point in bringing them all to me, which would probably give the man just the chance he needed to cover his tracks.

The partition wasn't more than fifty feet, probably not that long. When I rounded the end of it I could see the full extent of the floor down to the offices at the far end. I hurried away from that part of the building.

No one had missed me when with a gasp of relief I reached the door of the infirmary, where Peter and Smith had the others in a group. Peter had been asking questions and stopped just as I arrived.

"Where have you been?" he asked.

"Making a little tour of investigation," I replied. I drew him to one side and told him about the door at the end of the infirmary.

"I know," he said. "I went out that way. Whoever it was either escaped down the stairs or didn't leave the infirmary at all."

"Weren't any of them out of breath?" I asked.

He shook his head and countered with, "Was the doctor in the room with you?"

I remembered that the doctor came in directly behind Peter after the crash, and told him so. The doctor, of course, was a possibility, but I was inclined to think Peter was very wrong. I suppose a detective has to think of everything when a case gets as fogged as this one was at the moment. I was taxing what little mental powers I had left to find pieces to fit in the theory which I had been developing since the late afternoon. Peter had not said so, but I knew he still suspected Charlie and Beth. He wasn't satisfied of their innocence. Herbert, too, had come under his suspicions. I myself didn't like the idea of Herbert toting that gun around with him. It made me nervous. If

Herbert was guilty there was no telling what he might do if he thought he was finally trapped.

I tugged at Peter's sleeve and led him farther down the aisle. "Have you taken fingerprints of all these men?" I asked.

"I have," he replied.

"How about the plaque in Charlie's office which holds the darts, have you gone over that?"

He gave me an appreciative grin, but said nothing. I wanted to know badly if he had done that, but he offered no information. I asked no more questions. I've learned that you get more information out of people if you don't press them too hard.

It was a little after nine when the commotion finally subsided. I was frightfully tired, but wouldn't have admitted it for anything in the world. I'm proud and I'm vain about my fortitude at seventy-five and although I'd been under a strain all day I could see no reason why I shouldn't go on a bit longer. Peter had promised me a rest period which really was to be my time on duty. I slipped off to one side and sought the comforting embrace of a nice big soft chair. My bones ached a bit and I would have dozed off if I hadn't heard Sandy ask, "How much longer will the hunt last?"

"We won't catch him to-night," Peter replied. "We have a sick woman on our hands. You'll either have to go in a few minutes or else stay here all night."

"I'll stay if I can be of any help," Sandy offered

"Then you might as well make yourself comfortable for the moment." He turned to Smith and said, "Go through the offices and tell the men to clear out now or to be prepared to spend the night here in the store on this floor."

Smith wandered off. Davis was sound asleep on a day bed. Beth had moved over to a divan. None of the men were anywhere in sight. Peter went into the infirmary, intending, I suppose, to take a look at Mrs. Doyle.

I went over to sit beside Beth, she seemed so alone.

"What will happen now?" she asked.

"Just watch and wait," I replied.

"It doesn't seem real all this—" She made a nice expressive gesture with her hands.

"Do you think Carl was connected with the stock shortages?" I was blunt about it for a good reason. My idea had been developing and I wanted to get each phase of it in order.

"I'm afraid so," she admitted just as bluntly.

"But you're not sure?"

"No. He never told me. He hasn't worked for a long time, but he always had money. He had to get it from somewhere," she answered logically.

"Did he ever mention any one at the store familiarly —except girls?" I hastened to add.

"I know he saw Mr. Hastings once or twice," she replied.

Peter had just come out of the infirmary. I saw Herbert, looking like a lost soul, wandering down an aisle.

I excused myself and walked over to Herbert. I was more certain than ever that the crimes had been committed to hide something which had to do with the store.

I went with no spirit of braggadocio. I was a little tired and sick of it all. I had had a hard day, for me, and the tragedies had, if nothing else, given me a sense of the slight value of life. If it was a question of store management Charlie Doane had to be protected. I had lived my life to a ripe fullness and if bearding Herbert was going to mean the last act in the tragedy I think I was calmly willing to play that part as I sought Herbert. I for one didn't want to wait for the last move in the game if the thing could be cleared up quickly.

"Are you going home?" I asked Herbert as I approached him.

"No."

I didn't think he was, but his flat denial rather stumped me.

"What do you hope to do here?" I asked.

"What are you driving at?" he asked with considerable perception.

"I'd like to have these mysteries cleared up," I replied. "You could do it, couldn't you?"

He looked through me before he answered.

"You think I'm guilty, don't you?"

"I think you had opportunity and probably cause," I replied. "I'm positive that you, if you didn't kill all these people, could at least clear Charlie of Peter Conklin's suspicions and give Peter something more tangible to work on than he now has. As it is, he's playing a game of blindman's-buff. Why don't you tell him what you know?"

"Let Charlie worry about his own neck," he grumbled. "I'll take care of mine."

"Don't be careless with that gun," I warned. "There's been enough trouble to-day."

All the resentment Herbert had held back for years bubbled over and out of him. "Why don't you try minding your own business? You stick your nose into everything. Why don't you go home where you belong instead of trying to run the police department? Can't you keep your fingers out of other people's affairs? You're a meddlesome, disagreeable old woman who ought to have been dead years ago."

"If you committed these crimes you're at the end of your rope," I fired back at him. "If you didn't, you're a fool because you've been the tool of the murderer—but that's your funeral, not mine. Be pigheaded if you like; I was trying to help you."

"I don't want your help and I don't need it."

My departure could probably be called a flounce.

If you can take it, it does you good to get an unbiased view of yourself every once in a while. As I went back to Peter I was trying to decide whether or not Herbert was acting like an innocent man.

# CHAPTER NINETEEN

After an hour of waiting I was restless. There is nothing that wears you down like waiting for something to happen. The breathless calm before the storm has never been exaggerated, in my estimation. There was an air of expectancy about all of us on that floor except Davis, who with his glasses pushed up on his forehead snored spasmodically. Even Sandy, who dozed in a chair, seemed to possess the alert awareness of a sleeping cat. Charlie and Beth were sitting on a divan engrossed in nothing but themselves, so it seemed, but at the slightest sound they looked up quickly. Peter was buried in a big chair looking at some reports. Smith seemed uncomfortable sitting erect in a ladder-backed chair beside a grandfather's clock which, praise be, was not running.

I selected the chair next to Peter's and with a sigh settled down. He looked up for a second and went back to his reports, paying no further attention to me until he folded the papers and replaced them in his pocket.

"The hairs?" I asked.

He nodded.

"Anything definite?"

"Two suspects."

"Who?"

My eagerness and interest were ignored. "I can't tell you now," was all he said.

I was going to press him for the information, when the door of the infirmary opened and Mrs. Doyle's daughter came out and said, "She's ready."

"Is she going home?" I asked. I hated being left in the dark.

"No, she's coming out here," Peter said.

"What for?"

"To watch. I want her to spot our man for us."

"Peter, you can't do this. She may be killed," I protested vehemently.

"She'll be all right," he assured me.

"She wasn't safe a few minutes ago," I argued. "You're making a target out of her. It isn't fair. Herbert's roaming about this floor like a cat stalking its prey. He's carrying a gun. What's to prevent his shooting the woman?"

"Your nerves are going back on you. You'd better get some rest before your time on duty. I'll call you about one o'clock."

With that he left me, to reappear a few minutes later walking beside Mrs. Doyle, who was settled into a chair away from the lights. She was completely in the shadow, but the area near the infirmary door was well lit by the clever arrangement of bridge lamps which Peter had fixed with Mrs. Doyle's resting-place in mind.

"She'll be all right," he assured. "No one knows she's there but us."

"Where's Herbert?" I asked.

"He went back into his office a few minutes ago."

"And what is Mrs. Doyle supposed to do?" I asked.

"Just watch. She assured you she knew the man's back. I want her proof. That and the evidence of the hairs should tighten the noose about our man's neck."

"I'll never forgive myself or you if anything happens to her," I warned him.

"I wish you'd get some rest," he answered. "I'm depending on you later. You're to do duty with Davis. He's making sure of getting his sleep." A snore from Davis gave me ample proof of that.

Charlie and Beth were deeply engrossed in each other. Sandy still dozed. I didn't want to attract attention to Mrs. Doyle by talking to her. Peter was right. I was tired, dog tired, and the more I thought of it the more I wanted to rest. All the comfortable and available furniture near the infirmary was in use. I remembered a bed in one of the displays in the galleries. It was at the end of the aisle which ran across the building in front of the infirmary.

"I'm going over here," I said to Peter and started on my way.

"Where?" he asked.

"At the end of this aisle," I replied. "There are beds there all made up. I'll use one."

He grinned at me. I made no further explanation. If any one at any time had ever told me that I would relish a nap on a department store bed in one of their display galleries I would have been most contemptuous. As I went forward I had a very vivid picture of those little display rooms; some were done in maple and homespun, others in Empire or Victorian tradition, and still others dressed up in such a way with taffeta and frills to delight the heart of any harlot. If I picked one that was first-class Grand Rapids I didn't care, just so long as there wasn't one of those wax figures in the bed. They did that for reality. If there was a wax lady in the bed I picked she'd rest on the floor, because in my condition I was determined to take the first bed I found.

I groped my way about, ran into a silk cord which was stretched across the front of one of the deluxe displays, and finally found an unoccupied bed. I pulled back the silk coverlet, sat on the bed's edge to step out of my pumps and with a feeling of gratification lifted my legs up. Before I lay back I looked out at the floor. Through a tunnel of darkness I could see the spot of light near the infirmary entrance. I hoped, with a sigh, that Peter's plan would be successful. I stretched out on the bed, pulled the coverlet over me and went to sleep immediately.

I've heard all sorts of drivel about the ability to sleep. I don't know why I go to sleep when I go to bed. I don't have to read for ten minutes, neither do I find it necessary to count sheep or say the multiplication table. When I finally get into bed I go there for one purpose at my age—to sleep. I've heard people say it was a sign of a clear conscience. That may be true, but I think a well-trained imagination is of much more importance.

I don't know exactly how long I slept. I can remember thinking that a mattress was a little hard without a pad over it, because I was conscious of the buttons on the face of the mattress. I was thinking that perhaps I'd have button marks on me somewhere and remembered nothing more.

My sleep was not restful, because I began to dream. It was like looking into a kaleidoscope wherein the weird events of the day were jumbled in wild disorder. Faces, flashes of scenes, thoughts, reasons and motives swirled, taking shape clearly and distinctly for a moment and then vanishing just as quickly. It was like being caught in a wild raging torrent that mercilessly carried me with it. I fought trying to connect the faces and the scenes. I clutched at ideas, reasons and motives. I became frantic as I tried to fit the pieces together and unravel the tangled threads. The tempo increased, the movement became faster and faster until I was completely caught and rushed headlong toward some terrible and horrible pending disaster. I wanted to struggle because I was aware of my danger. I knew I was trying to call, but my throat was dry and no sound would come from my lips. There was no escape for me. I was going as all the others had gone that day. Resignation to a fate which I could not control paralyzed me. For a moment I seemed to be sinking and then suddenly, I knew I was no longer dreaming. I became wide awake, the resignation of my dream gone. Cold terror held me, enveloping me like an icy mold.

My eyes opened to a pitch-blackness charged with danger. Have you ever been unaccountably afraid? Do you know the terror of unexplainable fear? Have you ever been so terrified that you didn't dare blink an eyelash? I had known that fear before, but that is another story.

It wasn't because I was half awake or anything like that. I was wide awake when I opened my eyes to the impenetrable blackness. I knew I'd be able to see some reflection or glow from the lights in front of the infirmary if they were lit. There was no glow, neither was there the slightest sound. Where were the others? Why were they so quiet? What had happened to them all?

From somewhere out on the river I heard the dull throaty blast of a tugboat whistle. It is one of the nocturnal sounds of New York I've always loved. It reassured me and with that new assurance came other rational thoughts. Perhaps Peter had come quietly to waken me. I wanted more comfort than my thoughts. I wanted to hear my own voice. I was on the verge of calling softly when the words froze in my throat.

There was a movement beside my bed, a soft, barely perceptible movement of a foot sliding over a carpet. Instinctively I knew it was not Peter. Who was it and what did the person want?

I know I was as stiff as an icicle when an unseen hand took hold of the coverlet and pulled it away from me. My sense of humor helped me through that dreadful moment as I discarded the possibility of rape. This was no Sextus seeking a Lucretia. Most women have a strange pleasurable horror of being seized by bold predatory hands. It's natural that we should. It bucks up our vanity to think that we might be wanted that much.

There was a slight, barely audible grunt as my visitor leaned forward which made me visualize a paunch. I could feel hands on the mattress rather than hear them and knew what was going to happen. I was to be lifted from that bed and carried away. Why?

As the hands worked their way under me my thoughts raced. I didn't dare scream for fear I'd be strangled at once. There was no reason why any one should want this frayed, wrinkled, loose-skinned body of mine unless— The terror of my dream returned. I knew too much. It was to be my end. Whoever it was who had crept upon me knew I was there. My mouth and throat were just as dry as they had been in the dream. I was wishing for the blessing of free-flowing saliva when reason came. Suddenly it dawned on me. This man—I knew it was a man because of the stale smell of cigar smoke—had come for the body of Eva Sutton! In the darkness he had made a natural mistake.

It took every atom of control I possessed to keep from shuddering. It was exactly what Peter had predicted would happen. Why hadn't we discovered the body in one of the beds? Why had no one thought of that, unless the murderer had cleverly taken the galleries as his part of the search.

A new fear gripped me as I thought of Peter's question about the incinerator. Was that to be my end? Was the store equipped with chutes leading to the furnace similar to those seen in apartment houses? Was Peter watching? Would he save me? If I managed to cry out or struggle would I be killed for my effort and would the mysterious killer go free again?

I didn't know what to do. I'd heard different things about rigor mortis. Did the man know as much as I thought I did? I racked my memory and was sure that somewhere in my reading I had come across the information that a body stiffens after death and then becomes relaxed again. If Eva Sutton had been dead for several hours she should have passed through the stiffening process.

As the hands under me lifted there was another low grunt. I relaxed as much as I could. My head felt damned uncomfortable dangling down, as did the one arm which flopped over my side. I came within an ace of doing a stupid thing. I very nearly reached for my handbag as I felt my body leaving the bed. That's » something a good corpse would not do. I stopped the impulse just in time.

As my bearer turned, my foot slapped against some piece of furniture which very nearly made me cry out. As it was, I had a black and blue bruise there for weeks. With my head dangling I tried to see the portion of the floor which was exposed to my view. I could make out the outlines of windows on one side of the building and through one, way off in the distance, I could see an electric sign blinking on and off like some pulse of the night.

I had a bad jounce as the man stepped off the platform of the gallery and moved away. I'd have given anything in the world if I had known in which direction we were going. Where was Peter? Why didn't he do something? I was terrorized by a picture of seething hot flames. I gritted my teeth, which doesn't give you much satisfaction when you wear plates. It just hurts your gums a little.

As I was cautiously carried along an aisle a new fear took possession of me. Peter hadn't told me of his plans. Would he shoot at the man? There was no reason why he should not. You can't hurt a person who is already dead and he wouldn't know that I was not Eva Sutton.

He didn't know where the body had been hidden. There was no reason why he should be watching the galleries. I was in a dangerous position from any angle. Peter might shoot at the man and hit me or the man might drop me anywhere.

Since I have no desire to be cremated after I'm dead I decided then and there that I certainly wouldn't be burned alive. I'd wait until we were well out on the floor and then begin a scratching party to free myself I had an inward chuckle as I thought of the surprise my unknown carrier would feel when he discovered that he had crept upon and carried away something of live flesh and blood.

We stopped suddenly and I listened to determine why. I could feel the arms which held me tighten. I knew the man was listening, as I was, straining his ears for a sound.

Then I heard the voice. It wasn't a voice really; it was an audible breath which said, "So it's you."

It was Herbert speaking, I knew that, but if my life depended on my being sure, and it more or less did, I couldn't tell whether or not the voice came from the man who carried me.

"Don't be a fool," a second voice just as quiet said,

freighted with warning.

I wanted to scream or laugh or both. There were two men hissing like tomcats over me.

My bearer took a step to the side and it was that, I believe, which saved my life, for the next minute there was a most peculiar sound. A hissing and crackling going on under me. I have heard the children call them "son-of-a-guns." Anyhow, they are a sort of torpedo which cracks with minute explosions when they are stepped on. A variation of the old-style torpedo.

The sound startled both of us. I squirmed. I don't know what the man thought, but it must have been an awful shock, because he dropped me, right out of his arms, and I hit the floor with a nice flat flop on top of the snapping son-of-a-guns. I rolled over. The next instant there was the report and flash of a gun. I kept rolling and wound up under a day bed. During my rolling progress, there was a second gun-flash.

It all happened quicker than it takes to tell it. With my immediate danger over and feeling safe under the day bed I had a moment of uncontrolled hysteria and started to scream, long and loud; but my shrill voice was stilled by the sudden rush of lights which made me blink. I was looking upward and for a fraction of a second I saw the amazed distorted face of Herbert Hastings twisted in pain before it melted away from me.

I'm sure I fainted for at least thirty seconds. My next recollection was hearing excited voices calling from different parts of the store and the rushing of hurrying feet and the snapping of what seemed like hundreds of the son-of-a-guns. All the sounds were converging to the spot where I lay hidden under the day bed. I began to crawl out from under, sickened by what I saw. Herbert and John Grover were prone on the floor. I felt ill at the sight and was struggling up from my hands and knees when the others arrived. Charlie and Beth helped me to my feet and lowered me to a chair and then stood in front of me to save me from the horror which I had already seen. I pushed them aside so I could see what was going on.

The doctor was bending over Grover. Peter was kneeling beside Herbert. One of them was guilty, but which one?

"He's in a bad way," the doctor said, looking up. Then he set about stopping the flow of blood. He had a pair of shears which he used to cut Grover's coat away from his body. He pressed a pad over the wound and then said, "Carry him to the infirmary. Be careful." He crossed to Herbert.

Herbert's condition, too, was serious. The doctor shook his head doubtfully, while we watched, awed by the things which had happened.

"Is he dead?" Peter asked.

"No," the doctor replied. "We'll have to take him to the infirmary, too."

We all trailed along behind the body of Herbert, which Kramer and Sandy were carrying gingerly, passing Mrs. Doyle, who, tagged by her daughter, came toward us, a flannel ghost in that voluminous nightgown of hers.

# CHAPTER 20

Beth went in to help the doctor and was followed by Charlie.

"Well," Peter said. "It looks as if we have come to the end of the trail. How did you get mixed up in it?"

When I had explained my part in the drama he said, "You think Herbert or Grover thought you were the dead woman?"

I nodded.

"Then her body is still in one of those beds." He turned to Smith. "You and McLeod take a look."

Smith was back in a few minutes. The body was in the gallery next beyond the one I had used. Since they did use wax figures for display purposes it was an understandable reason for our not finding Eva when we looked for her.

"Which one of them carried you?" Peter asked.

"I don't know," I replied.

"Then we don't know yet," he said irritably. "I hope he confesses before he dies."

"Who?" I asked.

"Hastings," he answered.

"You're wrong," I snapped.

"Who told you?" he snapped back querulously.

"Nobody told me. I've been doing some thinking."

"Good. Then suppose you tell me why I'm wrong."

I don't know that he expected me to do it, but since I had a theory I decided to give it. I began back with the events of the early morning.

"We know that both Charles Doane and Herbert Hastings were in the little offices just before nine o'clock. Charles Doane didn't kill Mrs. Briggs, because he was seen by Mrs. Curtis going up the balcony stairs. If he had been guilty of murder he would have been more secretive about his actions. He left Herbert talking to Mrs. Briggs.

We don't know how Herbert left the offices, but we are sure of one thing, he did not go out via the back way. He very probably used the end exit into the store and was not seen. When the body of Mrs. Briggs was discovered, the murderer felt safe until we realized that it was not suicide but murder. The murderer probably knew that Herbert and Charlie both had been with Mrs. Briggs. The murderer also knew something which neither Charlie nor Herbert could know."

"What?" Peter asked, interested.

"The murderer knew that Willie, Carl Briggs and Eva Sutton had seen him enter that suite," I replied.

"Which doesn't eliminate Hastings from the picture," Peter reminded me.

"Yes, it does," I answered quickly and quite satisfied with myself. "Herbert Hastings entered the suite of offices before Eva Sutton met Carl Briggs. Herbert was in there talking to Mrs. Briggs when the murderer entered the wide corridor. The one thing I don't know or understand is why, since the murderer knew that Eva Sutton had seen him, he allowed her to live all day. We do know now, however, why she was afraid."

"And so?" Peter prompted me.

"The murderer knew he would have to eliminate dangerous witnesses, hence the doing away of Willie and the shooting of Carl Briggs. The man, as you said sometime before, knew all there was to know about the store. He watched for Carl Briggs. He stood in the whispering window and when he felt certain that Carl was about to expose him the shot was fired. There was only one person left who could closely identify him with the murder of Mrs. Briggs and that person was Eva Sutton. For some reason which we may never know, he felt sure of her.

"When I returned this afternoon with Mrs. Doyle, our murderer was listening at the window. He heard her talk about the gray suit. He was afraid of her identification and resorted to that crude attack on her life. He had heard the doctor say her heart was bad and he undoubtedly thought that a shock would be her finish."

"How about the dart in Mr. Doane's seat?" Peter asked seriously.

I knew exactly what he meant, but it did sound funny the way he said it.

"Our murderer wanted Mr. Doane out of the way so that the store meeting we were to have would be postponed temporarily if not indefinitely. Why, I don't know, but that will be the *raison d'etre* of the whole mad business.

"We know," I hurried on because I didn't want to be interrupted again, "that Eva Sutton came up here to see Herbert Hastings immediately after the store closed. That's why I feel our conversation signed her death-warrant."

"I tell you it had nothing to do with it," Peter insisted. It was very sweet of him to take that stand.

I went on. "The murderer had two things to worry about after having heard that conversation. Eva Sutton and the gray suit he was wearing."

"But after you went off to take your nap, all of the men passed Mrs. Doyle and she was unable to recognize any of them," Peter broke in.

"Naturally," I said, "because the murderer changed his suit."

"I'll be damned!" Peter muttered. I felt very smug, because I was sure he hadn't thought of that.

"Charlie Doane and Beth Oliver were hiding at the time I returned. Herbert Hastings was in his office talking to Eva Sutton. We know nothing of the whereabouts of Mr. Banter, Kramer or John Grover." I could see both Banter and Kramer squirm uncomfortably as eyes were turned in their direction.

"Which one is guilty?" Peter asked.

"John Grover," I replied, "and I'll tell you why I think so."

There was a sigh, of relief I imagine, from either

Banter or Kramer or both.

They were all leaning toward me raptly intent on what I was saying. I enjoy a good audience and since I had the stellar part I made the best of it. "This morning," I went on, "Grover rubbed a blotter along the edge of Mrs. Briggs' desk. Why? Because he was afraid he had left fingerprints there. When Sandy stopped the stretcher-bearers, it was Grover who was annoyed with him."

"That's right," Sandy said.

I flashed the young man a smile as I continued. "When I left to get Mrs. Doyle, Grover was in the wide corridor. We have no way of knowing how long he had been there, but he probably overheard our conversation and knew why I was going on my errand, which explains his being at the whispering window in the private office waiting for my return. I don't know what had happened between him and Eva Sutton. He was evidently afraid of her. He probably knew that she was up here and decided for safety's sake to do away with her. When I was looking for the hairs for you," I turned to Peter, "I saw a white thread inside the collar of Grover's coat, which bulged away from his neck a little. If you will send some one out there for the coat the doctor ripped off him I think you'll find that it was either a new suit or one which had just been cleaned. If you will go further and make a hunt for it, I bet you'll find a gray suit hidden somewhere in Grover's office or perhaps in the men's clothing department."

"The cut coat is here," Smith said, and handed it to Peter, who took the parts of it and held it gingerly because it was wet. Sure enough, on the inside of the collar there was the evidence of a tag having been hastily removed.

"I hand it to you," Peter said with admiration.

"If Herbert Hastings had been at the listening window he would have changed his suit," I said. "That's why I was sure it was not Herbert, but I knew it might have been either Mr. Banter or Grover."

Banter wiped his face and neck with evident relief.

"How did those torpedoes get out there on the floor?" I asked Peter.

"I put them there hoping they would betray any one who tried to prowl about," he explained.

"I believe they saved my life," I said.

"Praise God, you're safe!" Mrs. Doyle said with genuine feeling.

The doctor came to the door and beckoned to Peter, who, followed by Davis, entered the infirmary.

The others plied me with questions. We none of us could figure why Grover made the mistake he did. I will always believe that Grover dropped the silk rope in front of the gallery which held Eva's body so he could find it without a light. When he went groping his way through the dark he came to the rope which I had dropped to the floor when I bumped into it and believing that I was Eva, he lifted me and carried me off.

I don't know how long Peter was gone, because we talked and rehashed the events of the day, but when he came out and joined us he was very, very solemn.

"How are they?" I asked.

"Grover's dead. You were right."

"Then he confessed?"

"Enough. It's a bit garbled. Davis took it down. Grover wanted to get control of the store. He cultivated Hastings to get himself in here and then planted Eva Sutton as a vamp to get something on Hastings. Hastings fell for the girl and Grover then had him where he wanted him. Hastings didn't know all that was going on, Grover saw to that. Grover kept getting more and more power. He hoped to get the store in such shape that he could eventually buy it for next to nothing. Banter and Kramer were his chief aides. They had an elaborate thieving system which was controlled by Banter as personnel manager and Kramer as head of the store detectives. The thieving went on steadily.

That was one of Grover's ways of keeping the profits

down. The merchandise taken from the store was resold or stored until such time as Grover could use it at a handsome profit back here in the store. Grover put in a new system of bookkeeping and juggled figures. He didn't want public accountants called in, because his whole plot would be exposed. Hastings feared any scandal and as long as Grover could keep him quiet he felt reasonably safe.

"Mr. Doane's unexpected arrival complicated things, which explains the use of the dart Grover believed to be poisoned.

"When Grover heard of the suit which Carl Briggs threatened to bring against the store he had very little trouble making a lieutenant out of Briggs. Carl Briggs was one of the men who carried goods out of the store.

"When Mrs. Briggs called on her son last night her unexpected arrival threw a wrench in the works. She may have been suspicious, we'll never know about that, but she found jewelry in Carl's apartment which she knew should have been in the store. Mrs. Briggs threatened to spill the story this morning. Carl was panicked and telephoned Grover, who tried to reason with Mrs. Briggs this morning. He said he didn't mean to kill her. He wanted to put the fear of God, or the Devil, into her, I don't know which. He said he stepped behind her and seeing a loop of wire he put it about her throat and pulled. She gave just one convulsed jerk, that's when she broke the rosary, and died. The bottle of metal polish gave him the idea of making it look like suicide.

"He left through that little side door. He didn't remember what he did with the piece of wire."

"And I had it around me leg all day," Mrs. Doyle said, "and it had been used to kill a woman and all! The Saints preserve us!"

"He had to cover himself. He didn't trust Carl Briggs and he was afraid of Willie's testimony. We know what he did to them. He felt sure of the Sutton girl, however, because she had been in on the deal from the start. He did overhear our conversation when you returned this afternoon and met Eva Sutton just as she was coming out of Hastings' office and knowing that we suspected him she told Grover that he could count her out. She didn't intend to have Hastings framed. There was nothing for Grover to do then but put her out of the way. He strangled her and jammed her body into the chest. He went down to the clothing department and put on another suit. I guess that's all."

"Did he telephone Beth Oliver from the private office?" I asked.

"Yes," Davis cut in; "he did that to have an alibi for himself."

"Honors for solving the case go to Miss Thomas," Peter said. "I didn't know which of the two was guilty." He turned to me. "Both Hastings and Grover had hairs on their coats which matched those found in the box."

"It was really Eva Sutton who rounded out the case, wasn't it?" I asked.

"Yes. If she hadn't fallen for Hastings, he might have burned for these crimes. You can't figure on a woman," Peter said.

I could have slapped him. I can say things about other women because I happen to be a woman, but I won't have any man saying things about the loyalty of a woman to the man she loves. That girl gave her life for Herbert Hastings and I admire her for it.

"I guess you can all go home," Peter said wearily.

But the day was not over for me. The doctor came to the door and called me into the little room. "He wants to see you," he whispered in that sick-room tone we all use.

I couldn't imagine why Herbert had called me, of all people. We had had nothing in common through the years. I wonder if dying people have extra powers of perception. It made me uneasy to have him say as I stood beside him looking down,

"You're wondering why I asked for you, aren't you?" He stated it as a fact and not a question. His voice was weak.

There are times when words are utterly useless. I said nothing. I put my hand on his forehead, which looked hot.

"That feels good," he said. "I'm sorry for the things I said this afternoon."

"What things?" I barked at him. "I can't remember." My eyes felt full. Had the poor soul called me in to apologize before he died?

"You thought I was guilty, didn't you?" he asked.

"For a time I did," I replied.

"Will you help to cover the scandal?" he pleaded.

"There'll be no scandal. You shot that man in an effort to protect the Doane interests. When you're better if you have to appear in court, that's all you'll have to say."

"I'm not going to get better. I'm dying and I'm glad. I'm awfully tired, Miss Thomas. This afternoon when I blew up with you I thought I was through caring about the store and the name of Doane. You never liked me very much, I know that, but you weren't any different from the rest of them. They all treated me like an outsider just because I wasn't a Doane. At first I wanted to be as good as the Doanes; but nothing I did made any difference. I couldn't hurdle their wall."

While he rested I thought of the life he must have lived with Gladys and the Doane name. Poor devil, imagine wanting anything like that and eating your heart out because you couldn't get it.

"Do you know why I failed?" he asked.

I had a fairly good idea, but I didn't want to hurt his feelings.

"Why don't you tell me? You have a reputation for telling the truth no matter how much it hurts any one else."

There was no bitterness in his statement. "I'll tell you. It was because I was never myself. I was always trying to be a Doane."

I nodded my head in agreement.

"It took me a good many years to make that discovery,

and when I found it out it was too late," he added bitterly. "My best years were behind me and out of them I had nothing but my interest in the store and my failure to make myself as good as or equal to a Doane. A man has to have something to cherish. It sort of keeps him warm. I had nothing. Failures are cold things."

I had never thought of Herbert as a sensitive or a thoughtful person. As I stood there hearing his confession I knew how much I had misjudged him. There he lay, opening his heart to me with a freedom I was sure he'd regret if he lived. I wanted to stop him, but I did not dare. If he did die I'd be haunted by the memory of refusing him confession.

"I can talk to you," he went on, making me glad I had said nothing. "You've been around and done things. You're the only human one of the lot except Charlie and we never were able to get together. You're not a Doane, though; they think you're better than they are."

"That's absurd," I scoffed.

"Not to them," he insisted. "Family is important to them. They talk about you, don't quite approve of the things you do but they laugh them off because they don't dare say a thing, not even about what, in the bosom of the family, they called your scandalous escapades. I'm telling you this because I want somebody to understand about the girl. I loved her and I think she loved me."

"She did," I assured him. "She died because she loved you."

"I'm glad. Maybe we'll be together," he said hopefully. "She gave me the only happiness I've ever known and she was taken away from me. I'll see her, won't I?"

"Certainly," I lied valiantly I hope. It hurts to have a man show the emptiness of his life so completely when there is nothing you can say. Trite things are so damned ineffectual at one time and so pat at another. My eyes were smarting with unshed tears, my throat hurt.

"I didn't know about Grover and his plan to ruin the store until it was too late. He threatened to expose me. I couldn't have had a scandal. It would have spoiled all the things I had worked for for years. They didn't mean anything, but my reputation and connection with the store were all I had until I knew she really loved me. It's funny, isn't it," he asked, "the way you don't want to lose a thing even though you know it's no good?"

"We're all like that," I assured him, "hanging onto empty dreams most of the time."

"Then it isn't just me?" He seemed surprised.

"We're all alike under the skin."

"You won't let the scandal come out, will you?" he pleaded.

"I won't," I promised.

"You're a thoroughbred," he said and closed his eyes. I waited for a long time, but he said no more. I tiptoed to the door and called the doctor. "He's asleep," I whispered as the doctor came in. I waited.

After a moment's examination the doctor slowly pulled the sheet over Herbert's face. I could cry then and I did.

*****

This all happened months ago. You probably read some of it in the papers under the headlines of "The Bargain Day Murders." There was a great deal of it, as you can see, which, thanks to Peter, never did get into the papers.

Mrs. Doyle recovered fully and is now ensconced in my kitchen as cook, and an excellent one she is, too. She doesn't use the cook books I buy any more than the other one did. Both of her children married soon after her experience at the store and since I found myself without a cook I offered her the position. Now and then of an afternoon I go down to the kitchen for a cup of tea just to have a comforting talk with the poor soul.

Davis has been working with me on this book. If we sell it—and he says, "It would make a swell movie,"—he expects to take his share of the money and write something of his own.

Peter has been promoted for his skilful solution of the Bargain Day Murders. I see him now and then. He likes to drop ii for a chat and a drink. He wanted to swing credit for the case my way, but I wouldn't hear of that. He's young, he needs promotions since there is a young Conklin in the offing.

Beth and Charlie are married. I saw them off on their honeymoon, delayed a little until the affairs of the store could be straightened out. I gave Beth my share of Charlie's stock as a wedding-present and it really is a Doane store again.

I advanced Charlie enough money to tide the store over the first bad days. At first he didn't want to accept it, but when I told him he'd get my money eventually since I made him my chief heir years ago, he agreed.

They were very happy and when I left them at the boat on the eve of their departure, he told me he'd name his daughter after me.

"What if it's a boy?" I asked.

He answered me in less than a minute. "If it's a boy I'll call him Ethelbert," he grinned impishly.

"And if you do that," I flung back over my shoulder as I left them at the rail, "I'll disinherit all of you."

## THE END

# Resurrected Press Books in *The Chief Inspector Pointer Mystery* Series

## Murder at Bridge

When an afternoon bridge party attended by some of Hamilton's leading citizens ends with the hostess being murdered in her boudoir, Special Investigator Dundee of the District Attorney's office is called in. But one of the attendees is guilty? There are plenty of suspects: the victim's former lover, her current suitor, the retired judge who is being blackmailed, the victim's maid who had been horribly disfigured accidentally by the murdered woman, or any of the women who's husbands had flirted with the victim. Or was she murdered by an outsider whose motive had nothing to do with the town of Hamilton. Find the answer in... **Murder at Bridge**

## One Drop of Blood

When Dr. Koenig, head of Mayfield Sanitarium is murdered, the District Attorney's Special Investigator, "Bonnie" Dundee must go undercover to find the killer. Were any of the inmates of the asylum insane enough to have committed the crime? Or, was it one of the staff, motivated by jealousy? And what was is the secret in the murdered man's past. Find the answer in... **One Drop of Blood**

# AVAILABLE FROM RESURRECTED PRESS!

## THE EDWARDIAN DETECTIVES
## LITERARY SLEUTHS OF THE EDWARDIAN ERA

The exploits of the great Victorian Detectives, Poe's C. Auguste Dupin, Gaboriau's Lecoq, and most famously, Arthur Conan Doyle's Sherlock Holmes, are well known. But what of those fictional detectives that came after, those of the Edwardian Age? The period between the death of Queen Victoria and the First World War had been called the Golden Age of the detective short story, but how familiar is the modern reader with the sleuths of this era? And such an extraordinary group they were, including in their numbers an unassuming English priest, a blind man, a master of disguises, a lecturer in medical jurisprudence, a noble woman working for Scotland Yard, and a savant so brilliant he was known as "The Thinking Machine."

To introduce readers to these detectives, Resurrected Press has assembled a collection of stories featuring these and other remarkable sleuths in The Edwardian Detectives.

- The Case of Laker, Absconded by Arthur Morrison
- The Fenchurch Street Mystery by Baroness Orczy
- The Crime of the French Café by Nick Carter
- The Man with Nailed Shoes by R Austin Freeman
- The Blue Cross by G. K. Chesterton
- The Case of the Pocket Diary Found in the Snow by Augusta Groner
- The Ninescore Mystery by Baroness Orczy
- The Riddle of the Ninth Finger by Thomas W. Hanshew
- The Knight's Cross Signal Problem by Ernest Bramah

- The Problem of Cell 13 by Jacques Futrelle
- The Conundrum of the Golf Links by Percy James Brebner
- The Silkworms of Florence by Clifford Ashdown
- The Gateway of the Monster by William Hope Hodgson
- The Affair at the Semiramis Hotel by A. E. W. Mason
- The Affair of the Avalanche Bicycle & Tyre Co., LTD by Arthur Morrison

# RESURRECTED PRESS CLASSIC
## MYSTERY CATALOGUE

*Journeys into Mystery*
**Travel and Mystery in a More Elegant Time**

*The Edwardian Detectives*
**Literary Sleuths of the Edwardian Era**

*Gems of Mystery*
**Lost Jewels from a More Elegant Age**

**E. C. Bentley**
*Trent's Last Case: The Woman in Black*

**Ernest Bramah**
*Max Carrados Resurrected:*
*The Detective Stories of Max Carrados*

**Agatha Christie**
*The Secret Adversary*
*The Mysterious Affair at Styles*

**Octavus Roy Cohen**
*Midnight*

**Freeman Wills Croft**
*The Ponson Case*
*The Pit Prop Syndicate*

**J. S. Fletcher**
*The Herapath Property*
*The Rayner-Slade Amalgamation*
*The Chestermarke Instinct*
*The Paradise Mystery*
*Dead Men's Money*

*The Middle of Things*
*Ravensdene Court*
*Scarhaven Keep*
*The Orange-Yellow Diamond*
*The Middle Temple Murder*
*The Tallyrand Maxim*
*The Borough Treasurer*
*In the Mayor's Parlour*
*The Saftey Pin*

**R. Austin Freeman**
*The Mystery of 31 New Inn from the Dr. Thorndyke
Series*
*John Thorndyke's Cases from the Dr. Thorndyke
Series*
*The Red Thumb Mark from The Dr. Thorndyke Series*
*The Eye of Osiris from The Dr. Thorndyke Series*
*A Silent Witness from the Dr. John Thorndyke Series*
*The Cat's Eye from the Dr. John Thorndyke Series*
*Helen Vardon's Confession: A Dr. John Thorndyke
Story*
*As a Thief in the Night: A Dr. John Thorndyke Story*
*Mr. Pottermack's Oversight: A Dr. John Thorndyke
Story*
*Dr. Thorndyke Intervenes: A Dr. John Thorndyke
Story*
*The Singing Bone: The Adventures of Dr. Thorndyke*
*The Stoneware Monkey: A Dr. John Thorndyke Story*
*The Great Portrait Mystery, and Other Stories: A
Collection of Dr. John Thorndyke and Other Stories*
*The Penrose Mystery: A Dr. John Thorndyke Story*
*The Uttermost Farthing: A Savant's Vendetta*

**Arthur Griffiths**
*The Passenger From Calais*
*The Rome Express*

**Fergus Hume**
*The Mystery of a Hansom Cab*
*The Green Mummy*
*The Silent House*
*The Secret Passage*

**Edgar Jepson**
*The Loudwater Mystery*

**A. E. W. Mason**
*At the Villa Rose*

**A. A. Milne**
*The Red House Mystery*
**Baroness Emma Orczy**
*The Old Man in the Corner*

**Edgar Allan Poe**
*The Detective Stories of Edgar Allan Poe*

**Arthur J. Rees**
*The Hampstead Mystery*
*The Shrieking Pit*
*The Hand In The Dark*
*The Moon Rock*
*The Mystery of the Downs*

**Mary Roberts Rinehart**
*Sight Unseen and The Confession*

**Dorothy L. Sayers**
*Whose Body?*

**Sir William Magnay**
*The Hunt Ball Mystery*

**Mabel and Paul Thorne**
*The Sheridan Road Mystery*

**Louis Tracy**
*The Strange Case of Mortimer Fenley*
*The Albert Gate Mystery*
*The Bartlett Mystery*
*The Postmaster's Daughter*
*The House of Peril*
*The Sandling Case: What Would You Have Done?*
*Charles Edmonds Walk*
*The Paternoster Ruby*

**John R. Watson**
*The Mystery of the Downs*
*The Hampstead Mystery*

**Edgar Wallace**
*The Daffodil Mystery*
*The Crimson Circle*

**Carolyn Wells**
*Vicky Van*
*The Man Who Fell Through the Earth*
*In the Onyx Lobby*
*Raspberry Jam*
*The Clue*
*The Room with the Tassels*
*The Vanishing of Betty Varian*
*The Mystery Girl*
*The White Alley*
*The Curved Blades*
*Anybody but Anne*
*The Bride of a Moment*
*Faulkner's Folly*
*The Diamond Pin*
*The Gold Bag*
*The Mystery of the Sycamore*
*The Come Backy*

**Raoul Whitfield**
*Death in a Bowl*


*And much more!*
*Visit ResurrectedPress.com*
*for our complete catalogue*

## About Resurrected Press

A division of Intrepid Ink, LLC, Resurrected Press is dedicated to bringing high quality, vintage books back into publication. See our entire catalogue and find out more at www.ResurrectedPress.com.

## About Intrepid Ink, LLC

Intrepid Ink, LLC provides full publishing services to authors of fiction and non-fiction books, eBooks and websites. From editing to formatting, from publishing to marketing, Intrepid Ink gets your creative works into the hands of the people who want to read them. Find out more at www.IntrepidInk.com.